POWERFUL MEDICINE

A JOHNNY GERONIMO MYSTERY

GARY ROBINSON

Tribal Eye Productions
Santa Ynez, California

ISBN-13: 978-0-9800272-2-8

DEDICATION

*This book is dedicated to my best friend
and life partner, Lola, who inspires me
and reminds me of the important
things in life.*

CONTENTS

ACKNOWLEDGMENTS

There are several things I'd like to acknowledge.
These are things not necessarily found on most acknowledgment
pages written by authors at the front of their books.
I acknowledge that Santa Fe, New Mexico, is one of my
favorite places in America. I acknowledge that Native American
reservations are also favorite places of mine. In addition,
I recognize that many mysterious phenomena occur in our world
that most people consider spooky or unbelievable, but that is
because most people don't really understand how this world works
or what is really going on here. That's too bad, because a
little more open-mindedness could go a long way towards
ending religious, racial and other social disagreements. And
thus ends my acknowledgments, for now.
-*the author*

1 Chapter One

To Johnny Geronimo, Monday mornings felt fresh—filled with new possibilities and even maybe second chances. At least that's what he liked to think as he walked the few blocks from his pseudo-adobe apartment to his downtown office overlooking the main plaza of Santa Fe.

The feeling was always fleeting, but he allowed it to engulf him along with the crisp, high desert air.

An integral part of this Monday morning ritual was a stop at the corner of Palace and Lincoln to buy a copy of the <u>Santa Fe New Mexican</u> newspaper, and today was no different. Reading through the window of the vending machine, he scanned the front page headline: RECORD CROWDS EXPECTED FOR THIS YEAR'S INDIAN ART MARKET. This was a predictable headline for an August day in Santa Fe. It's probably the same headline the newspaper had run every year on this day for at least the last twenty-five years.

True, Johnny thought, the <u>Santa Fe New Mexican</u> was an over-priced, small town rag, but it was no ordinary over-priced, small town rag. It reflected the point of view of the locals, the real locals: the Latinos, American Indians and Anglos who'd put down roots here long ago—not the crop of New Age, art-dealing celebrities who'd invaded the town in the last half of the twentieth century. So what if it wasn't the voice of trendy urban enlightenment.

He put seventy-five cents in the slot, reached in and grabbed the top copy. Folding it, he tucked it under his arm and took in breath of fresh morning air. Following his ritual path, he strolled toward the *portale* of the Palace of the Governors.

The Palace of the Governors was Santa Fe's number one tourist destination. Built in 1610 by the Spanish colonial army, it originally housed the ruling elite who governed this once-remote outpost of the Spanish empire.

It also served to protect the colonists from so-called "Indian uprisings" and such. But, for at least a hundred years, you could find thirty or more American Indians from the nearby Pueblos selling their finest jewelry, pottery and baskets along the Palace Avenue sidewalk.

"Hey, Patch!" a familiar voice rang out from the line of Native vendors, addressing Geronimo by his well-known nickname.

"Victor! Mi compadre. How's business?"

Patch stopped for a moment to visit with this old friend from San Juan Pueblo.

Many of the vendors knew Patch. He was an easy-going, likable guy, and he'd loaned most of them a few bucks or helped them out of a jam one time or another.

As Patch talked, his eyes roamed the crowd of gathering tourists. He was always on the lookout for some young lovely in town for a few days who might be in need of a guide to show them the streets and secrets of Santa Fe. Secrets. Santa Fe had plenty of those.

And the women couldn't keep their eyes off of Patch, either. Who could blame them? With his straight jet-black hair and smooth, brown skin, this handsome, thirty year-old Apache was in his prime. Today he looked especially fine—more like a Southwest icon than usual—with his western cut sports jacket and faded blue denim shirt, unbuttoned at the top. His bolo tie loosely dangled from the collar.

"How about you?" Victor asked. "Sold any of your stuff lately?"

"No,"Patch replied. "I don't know what the problem is. I've got three unfinished paintings gathering dust in the corner of my studio, and two silver jewelry pieces just waiting for a final polish.'

"It happens, man," Victor said. "Don't sweat it. It'll pass."

"I'm glad I didn't quit my day job," Patch joked. "Anyway, good luck. Indian Market will be here in just a couple of weeks, and the tourists ought to be easy pickin's."

Victor chuckled and nodded as Patch resumed his trek.

Crossing the street, he cut diagonally through Santa Fe's historic plaza. In the center of the plaza stood a familiar landmark, a stone obelisk erected by civic-minded Anglos proud of the survival of their race here in the desert southwest.

The words originally etched into its base told you that it had been dedicated to the memory of those who served in the U.S. army and lost their lives at the hands of "savage" Indians. In a more recent, quasi-enlightened era, someone had carefully obliterated the word "savage," but everyone knew what it used to say. Patch had always thought it was a remarkable and curious monument of a confused culture.

He surveyed the Plaza, which was filled with the usual summer mix: tourists, locals and an international assortment of care-free young people skateboarding, strumming guitars or just laying back in the grass.

As he reached the far side of the Plaza, he looked up toward the window of his second story office. Painted on the glass for all the world to see were the words: EAGLE EYE INVESTIGATIONS: J. GERONIMO AND WILLARD CHINO, PARTNERS.

The light was on inside, and he knew his secretary, Jessie, was on the job. He smiled. He loved how he could always count on her.

Patch paused at the outdoor espresso cart on the sidewalk, his last stop before mounting the stairs to his office and beginning the workday. The girl behind the cart knew what Patch wanted: one double-tall mocha latte to go. That combination of caffeine and chocolate—what a way to kick-start the day.

With paper and espresso in hand, he walked the few steps to Number 76 East San Francisco Street. These numbers, printed in gold above the rather plain wood and glass door, was the only visible evidence of the offices located upstairs above the Overland Sheepskin Company. Patch opened the door and headed up the creaky set of wooden stairs.

Built in 1898, the building had witnessed a lot of history—"colorful history" according to the tourist brochures. Patch considered himself fortunate to have his office in such a prestigious location, facing on the world-famous Santa Fe Plaza and all.

The building's owner, D. B. "Dub" Anderson, had readily agreed to let Patch have the office space rent-free in exchange for sleuthing services. The deal had given Patch instant credibility with the downtown business community, which, it turned out, had an amazing amount of personal "dirty laundry" to be investigated or protected, depending on your point of view. In any case, finding out what had been going on behind some of Santa Fe's most private and elite doors had become Patch's bread and butter business.

Patch rounded the corner at the top of the stairs only to find Victoria Stanford blocking his path. The eccentric and wealthy elderly woman was burning a bundle of sage and wafting the smoke around the hallway.

Geronimo turned away, hoping she hadn't seen him. Too late. Her smile revealed her delight in catching him off guard.

"Ah, Geronimo, there you are," she said. "Please step into my office, won't you?"

She continued wafting the smoke as she walked.

"What are you doing, Victoria?" Patch inquired.

"You know perfectly well what I'm doing. Smudging - the whole building."

She entered her office, beckoning Patch to follow. Reluctantly, he stepped inside. A cultural clashing of Victorian opulence and Santa Fe style, the spacious room was filled with the trappings of a New Age enthusiast.

The sacrifices he's had to make to stay in business, Patch thought. He'd become partners with the enemy, so to speak. Thankfully, she was a *silent* partner.

"Of course I know what smudging is, but what's the occasion for the cleansing?" Patch asked. "Getting ready for one of your séances?"

"You'll be on your own for a couple of weeks," she replied. I'm going to India with Sri Ananda."

"You mean Ira Kowalski?" Patch blurted incredulously.

"That was his identity in a former manifestation of his life. Don't make fun of what you don't understand."

"Well, have a great trip," Patch offered as he headed for the door. "I've got to get to work."

"Wait, Patch." She approached him, took the newspaper and coffee cup from him and placed them on her desk. She took his hands and held them in hers.

"I did a reading on you last night. You need to be careful in the next few days. There's a Scorpio-Gemini conjunction coming on your next case."

"Translation?"

"Keep your pants zipped, and your eagle eye open for twins," she replied. "They'll play a prominent role."

Momentarily, he searched his memory banks looking for a suitable place to file this strange and seemingly irrelevant information.

"Okay, thanks, Vic. Consider me enlightened."

Kissing her on the cheek, he turned again to leave.

"Happy jet trails. Gotta go."

He winked as he picked up his coffee and paper. In a flash, he was out of there.

A few more steps down the second story hall took Patch to his office. As he entered his outer office reception area, Jessie was just closing the door to his private inner office.

Jessie was a sweet girl, a misplaced urban Comanche who'd come to study art at Santa Fe's Institute of American Indian Art. It was after struggling in two years of classes that she discovered that she really wasn't an artist. Now in her late twenties, Patch thought of this attractive woman almost as a younger sister. It was better that way.

She and Patch were alike in a lot of ways. Neither of them had continued practicing the tribal cultures they'd been raised with. And each of them only spoke a few words of their own native language. They were sort of tribal orphans in a way, trying to move beyond their own indigenous roots. Redefining what it meant to be an American Indian in an ever-changing modern America. Maybe that's why they worked well together.

"Good morning, Jessie dear," Patch said merrily.

"Someone's waiting in your office to see you," his secretary responded rather matter-of-factly. "In a bad way, too, I'd say. The name's Barkley."

"A client?" he asked hopefully.

"I suppose," Jessie replied with an air of feigned indifference.

"A cheating spouse?" Patch said, ignoring her attitude.

"Missing person, I think," Jessie said, picking up a nail file. "Anyway, you'll want to see for yourself. She's just your type. Female."

Jessie's sarcasm could be as dry as the New Mexico desert air.

"Then step aside, Jessie dear. Times a-wastin'."

Patch put the coffee cup and newspaper down on Jessie's desk, buttoned his top shirt button and straightened his bolo tie. Leaving the newspaper behind, he picked up the coffee cup and took a sip. He sauntered to his office door and opened it.

Peering into his inner sanctum, the private eye looked the woman over before he spoke. She was a gorgeous, thirty-something blonde, poured nicely into a tight-fitting white dress. He turned back and winked at Jessie.

"Sorry to keep you waiting, Ms. Barkley," he said, entering and closing the door behind him. "I'm John Geronimo."

As he crossed the room, her troubled eyes studied him nervously. She rose from her chair to greet him.

"Thank you for seeing me, Mr. Geronimo," she said with a slight quiver in her voice. Patch shook her hand, then motioned for her to be seated. She sat on the edge of the chair, anxiety written all over her pretty face.

Patch walked around the corner of his worn, wooden desk and sank into a large, over-stuffed leather chair that had seen better days. Everything in this office had seen better days.

Opening the top drawer, he took out a pouch of tobacco and some rolling papers.

"Now what can I do for you, Ms. Barkley?"

He began rolling a cigarette. Nervously, she took a deep breath. As she started to speak, her sense of panic emerged.

"It doesn't make any sense to me," she said. "I've come all this way, and I can't find her. I don't know what to do."

She bit her lip and turned her head away from Patch. A tear welled up at the corner of one eye, and she rummaged around in her handbag until she came up with a tissue.

"There, there, Ms. Barkley," Patch said in a calming tone of voice. "I'm sure it can't be all that bad. Why don't you take a deep breath, and start at the very beginning."

She took a deep breath, then exhaled.

"That would be San Francisco," she said in a much more relaxed tone.

"Okay," Patch replied. "Let's begin in San Francisco."

"It's my sister, Millie."

Now her words begin to tumble out.

"She's younger than I am, only eighteen. She met this guy. I don't know where, we don't hang out at the same places, you know. Our parents are away in Hong Kong. It would kill them if they found out. I've got to get her home before they come back."

Patch nodded as if all this made perfect sense.

"Go on," he said patiently.

"They're coming home the first of next month," she continued.

"That gives us about two weeks," Patch calculated.

She was on a roll and kept going.

"I didn't have any idea what was going on until her letter arrived. Then I didn't know what to do. I was frantic. What could I do?"

She was almost pleading with Patch to approve of her actions. He obliged. He'd learned that part of being a private eye also meant being a good listener, like a bartender.

"Probably nothing," he reassured her. "But, after her letter came, then what?"

Again, the words tumble out.

"She wouldn't answer my calls or texts, so I sent her a telegram asking her to come home. I addressed it to the La Fonda Hotel here in Santa Fe. That was the only address she had given me.

"I waited a whole week, but no answer came. So I decided to come out here to get her myself. I wrote her that I was coming. I guess that wasn't so smart, was it?"

Patch was putting the pieces together in his mind.

"It's not always easy to know what to do. So you haven't found her?"

"No, I haven't."

The blonde was quickly regaining her composure.

"I wrote in my letter that she should meet me in the hotel coffee shop, just to talk. I waited for three days. She never came. No message. Nothing."

Patch's mind began to wander.

"Uh-huh," he replied, absent-mindedly.

"It's been horrible!"

Ms. Barkley burst into tears again.

"Just waiting like this. Not knowing what's happened to her, or where she is."

She paused a moment to compose herself once again.

"I wrote her another letter since I got here, and left it at the front desk. I waited around in the lobby yesterday until it closed. She never came."

"It must've seemed hopeless at that point," Patch remarked.

"Yes. I waited there again this morning, but there was no sign of Millie. But I saw that man, Jonathan Morgan. He's behind all of this. I'm sure."

Patch's mind snapped back into focus.

"He wouldn't tell me where Millie was," the blonde said angrily. "He wouldn't tell me anything except that she was right where she wanted to be."

The fear in her voice began to return.

"But he'd say that anyway, wouldn't he?"

"Probably," Patch said dispassionately.

"But he said she didn't want to see me," she continued. "I know that can't be true. Anyway, he said he'd bring her to the hotel this evening to see me, if she wanted to. He doubted that she'd want to. But he did say he would come on his own, even if she didn't want to."

Just then, the office door opened. Ms. Barkley was startled by the interruption. A heavy-set Native American man with a boyish demeanor came into the room a step.

"Oh, excuse me," he said politely. Hastily removing his hat, he began to back out the doorway.

"It's all right, Willy," Patch said. "Come in."

The man stepped all the way in.

"Ms. Barkley, this is my partner, Willard Chino. Willy."

Willy bowed slightly to Ms. Barkley and smiled as he shut the door behind him. Willy, a thirty-year-old Pueblo Indian with short cropped hair and a faded brown suit, held a half-eaten donut. Self-consciously, he stashed the donut in his jacket pocket. Then, awkwardly, he leaned back against the door. Willy's boyish manner seemed to show itself most around beautiful women.

Patch launched into his interpretation of Ms. Barkley's story for Willy.

"Ms. Barkley's sister, Millie, ran away from San Francisco with a man named Jonathan Morgan. They're somewhere here in Santa Fe. Ms. Barkley bumped into Morgan and has set up a meeting with him tonight. We hope he'll bring her sister with him. Chances are good that he won't. Ms. Barkley wants us to find her sister, get her away from Morgan and back home."

He looked to Ms. Barkley. "Is that about right?"

"Yes, Mr. Geronimo. That is right."

Willy listened intently, trying to take it all in: the information Patch was telling him and the beautiful Ms. Barkley. He stared blankly at Patch.

Patch tried again.

"It's simple, really," he said. "One of us has to be at the hotel tonight to shadow Morgan when he leads us to Ms. Barkley's sister. If she doesn't want to go with us after we've found her—well, there are ways of accomplishing this."

Willy got the picture.

"Okay, yeah," he said, smiling.

Ms. Barkley looked up. There was fear on her face.

"But you've got to be careful," she said. "I'm afraid of what he might do to Millie. He might hurt her or something."

Patch smiled, reached over and pat Ms. Barkley's arm reassuringly.

"Don't you worry," he told her. "Just leave everything to us. We know what to do."

"But you've got to realize that Morgan may be a dangerous man," she retorted. "I don't think he'd give it a second thought if he had to hurt Millie to save himself."

"I thought you didn't know him very well," Patch reminded her.

Ms. Barkley blushed in confusion.

"It's just a feeling I got. You know, woman's intuition."

Patch nodded his head.

"Yeah, I know plenty about that."

He reached for a pad and pencil.

"So what does this Morgan look like?"

"He has blonde hair and fair skin," she said, looking out the window thoughtfully.

Patch jotted down the description.

"Very Nordic looking," she continued. "He talks loud and gives the impression of being, well... violent."

"How's he built?" Patch queried. "Thin, medium, heavy?"

"Muscular," she replied. "Broad-shouldered. Kind of a military-type man. He was wearing an expensive-looking leather overcoat when I saw him this morning."

"And what time are you meeting him?"

"Around eight."

He put down the pencil.

"All right, Ms. Barkley. One of us will be there."

"I'll look after it personally," Willy said.

"Thank you, both, so much. I can't tell you what this means to me."

She opened her handbag, brought out three $100 bills and put them on the desk.

"Will that be enough?" she asked.

Patch stood up and nodded.

"That should about cover it," he said.

She offered her hand, and as Patch took it she said, "Thanks, again."

Patched looked at the money.

"It's our pleasure," he smiled. "Now you be sure to meet Morgan in the lobby."

"I will," she said with a sigh of relief.

"I'll be there, too," Willy reassured her. "You won't need to look for me. I'll see you."

She nodded. Patch walked her to the door. She left with just one last glance back at Patch.

After closing the door, Patch returned to his desk. Willy was examining one of the bills. He handed the others to Patch.

"I just love dead presidents," Willy said with a mischievous grin. "Especially fat ones."

He folded the bill and stuffed it in his front pocket.

"Enough for frybread and posole for a week," he quipped and patted the pocket holding the bill.

Patch placed the others in a metal lock box in the lower drawer of his desk.

"Whata'ya think of the lady?" he asked jokingly.

"Bitchin' babe," Willy exclaimed. "Bet she's got boyfriends lined up around the block."

He poked his chest with pride.

"But I'm the one meeting her tonight."

Patch chuckled as Willy put on his hat and headed for the door.

"This ought to be a piece of cake, Willy," Patch said with a smile. "But watch your back anyway. Okay, partner?"

"Sure thing," Willy replied with a nod and left the room.

Patch swiveled his chair toward the window and gazed out at the Plaza. He ran Ms. Barkley's story over in his mind. There was something odd here, but he couldn't put his finger on it. He lit his cigarette. Oh well, he thought. It will be revealed. It always is.

2 Chapter Two

There's a certain hill north of downtown Santa Fe just a few blocks from Patch's apartment. It's called the Hill of the Martyrs. On top of the hill stands a huge white cross, a monument to a few Spanish Catholic priests who died during the Pueblo Revolt of 1680 when the Pueblo Indians evicted their uninvited guests from the region.

Patch thought it was strangely sad that there wasn't a similar monument to the eighty Pueblo Indian martyrs who were put to death when the Spaniards retook the territory twelve years later in the so-called "bloodless" re-conquest.

Of course, Patch was the first to admit that he had a sort of love-hate relationship with Santa Fe. The Hill of the Martyrs was one of those places that reminded him of that.

Nevertheless, he couldn't deny that it was one of the best places to watch a Santa Fe sunset. There was a certain mysterious feeling that crept over you as the late afternoon light painted both earth and sky with those fantastic orange, pink and magenta hues. That's just the feeling Patch was looking for tonight as the sunset's drama played out before him.

Evening descended once again on the fairytale town called Santa Fe, with its intoxicating and mysterious magic. But danger sometimes lurked under the cloak of darkness. Even here.

Shortly after eight p.m., Willy was on the job, tailing the man called Jonathan Morgan who had appeared punctually at the appointed time and place. Barkley and Morgan had interacted briefly in the hotel lobby, then separated. There had been no sign of this Millie. Curious, Willie thought.

Morgan was now taking a back alley route down a dark, narrow street named DeVargas, just off the Old Santa Fe Trail. All Willy could see in the moonlight was the shadow of his target moving past the row of old adobes.

Suddenly, a second figure stepped out of the shadows in front of Morgan. The two figures seemed to struggle momentarily. A scream echoed down the street. Willy ran towards the pair. Only a brief flash of light reflected off dark metal warned that a gun had been drawn. Two quick shots rang out in the quiet darkness. Two bullets struck an unsuspecting Willard Chino square in the chest.

With a gasp and a moan, Willy dropped to the ground. The shooter looked down at the body, and, after making sure that no one saw, crept back into the shadows. The other figure ran down the street into the darkness, abandoning the innocent body sprawled on the pavement.

Only Willy's ancient Native ancestors remained to watch his life ooze out on the black asphalt in a modern world not of their making.

A short time later, Patch was just entering his first dream cycle for the night. In the dream, he was painting a canvas, adding a few strokes to the tan wall of an adobe building. Suddenly, dark red paint began to ooze from the center of the wall. Patch tried wiping it away, only succeeding to smear the red liquid all over the canvas. A panic gripped him. He rubbed the spreading red blotch furiously, trying to obliterate any trace of its fearful presence. As he rubbed, he became aware of a ringing in his ear. The dream faded as Patch awoke to the ringing of his phone.

In the semi-darkness of his bedroom, he sat up in bed. Soft moonlight streamed in through his window, illuminating the ringing cellphone on the night stand. He picked it up after the fourth ring.

"Yes?" Patch answered groggily. "Yes, this is John Geronimo. Yes, Yes, he's my partner. What?" His mind snapped into sharp focus.

"Say again... How? ...You're sure it's Willy... Intensive care, St. Vincent's. Where'd it happen? Okay, I'll be right there...Um, is he gonna make it? I understand. Thanks." He clicked off the call.

"Willy, Willy, Willy," Patch said out loud. "What have I gotten you into?"

He switched on the table lamp and surveyed his *placita*. The rather small guest house had been a relatively good deal, at least for the Santa Fe renter's market. Larger than an efficiency, but not quite a one bedroom, the cosy quarters were part of the price you paid for living in quaint downtown Santa Fe. At least it was close enough to his office to walk to work each day.

He studied his art "studio" for a moment, really just one corner of the apartment. A large unfinished abstract painting of a lone American Indian figure against an urban cityscape stood on an easel. Two other similar unfinished pieces leaned against a wall.

Barefoot and wearing a pair of sweat pants with no top, Patch looked at the digital alarm clock on the night stand. It read 2:30 am. Next the clock was a copy of the book Apache Leaders of the 1800s.

Patch ran his hands through his hair a couple of times and reached for a packet of cigarette papers and a bag of tobacco beside the phone. He rolled a cigarette and put it in his mouth.

Before lighting it, he used the speed dial code on his phone to call a cab. Then he stood up and paused motionless for a couple of beats.

He walked slowly, but deliberately, across the room to the built-in kitchen in the corner. Opening a cupboard, he withdrew a glass. Then from the cabinet under the sink, he extracted a bottle of gin. Pouring himself a shot, he proceeded to down it, forgetting about the unlit cigarette already in his mouth.

All he managed to do was dunk the cigarette in the gin. This startled him, causing him to spill the contents of the glass down the front of himself and on the floor. With a big sigh and a loud "Shit," he retrieved a dish towel from the counter and wiped himself and the floor.

He decided that having a drink right now was not in the cards. He replaced the bottle in the cabinet, put the glass in the sink and wiped the up the precious liquid he'd spilled.

He walked to his closet, opened it, peered in and removed a shirt. Dressing himself, he headed out into the cool night air and the waiting cab.

One end of the block-long DeVargas Street dead-ended at Old Santa Fe Trail, almost right in front of San Miguel, America's Oldest Church. At least that's what the travel brochures said. Patch knew that when it came to churches, the Hopi and Pueblo plazas had the Catholics beat be at least five thousand years.

As Patch stepped out of the taxi, he saw a handful of police cars parked at the entrance to the narrow little street. It had been taped off with yellow, crime scene police tape. The area was lit by a bright, portable light. Several cops milled around. A camera flashed from down in the alley.

As Patch began to step under the yellow tape and enter DeVargas, a uniformed cop blocked his way.

"Hold it," the officer said. "You can't go in there."

"I'm John Geronimo," Patch protested. "Detective Sam Roybal called me down here."

The officer relaxed.

"Okay, go on back," he said. "But be careful where you step. There's a lot of blood back there."

Patch glared at him for a heartbeat. It was Willy's blood the cop was talking about. The Apache stepped under the yellow tape and strode down the alley.

The narrow alley was lined on both sides with old adobe buildings butted up one against one the other, a reminder of Santa Fe's humble roots. Patch walked down to where both uniformed and plain clothes policemen were clustered. He stepped into the circle of men. In the center was a large chalk outline drawn on the pavement where a body used to be. A large pool of dark drying blood covered the chest area on the pavement.

Patch knelt down next to the outline, reached down and touched the blood stain. He rubbed a little of the blood between his fingers. Willy's blood. A pair of blue jeans and cowboy boots stepped into the circle next to Patch.

"Hello, Patch," said the man wearing the jeans and boots.

Patch looked up in the direction of the voice, then stood up.

"Hello, Sam," Patch said to Lt. Roybal. Roybal was a short, stocky, Columbo-type Hispanic man with a mustache, wearing an unbuttoned trench coat. Patch and Roybal had known each other for several years.

"I figured you'd want to see this before we cleared the site," Roybal said in a gentle way.

"Thanks."

Patch appreciated the courtesy Roybal had offered him.

"Any sign of a struggle?" he asked.

"No," Roybal replied.

He turned to the other officers standing in the circle.

"All right. Get on with the search."

The circle broke up.

He turned back to Patch.

"Whoever did it fired close enough to leave powder burns on Willy's coat," the cop explained in an efficient policeman-like tone. "And the hundred dollar bill in his coat pocket seems to rule out robbery as a motive."

Patch flipped a switch in his mind that turned on his investigative mode. It was the only way to get through this.

"Who found him?" he asked.

"Albright over there," Roybal said, pointing to a young cop who was searching the bushes for clues.

"His regular beat."

"Anybody hear the shot?" Patch asked.

"Don't know yet," Roybal answered. "We just got here ourselves. Was Willy working on something?"

"Yeah."

Patch's response was guarded. He didn't want to say more than he absolutely had to.

"He was supposed to be trailing a guy named Jonathan Morgan."

"What for?"

Patch had said enough for tonight.

"Nothing really. Listen, I'm gonna get over to the hospital and then go break the news to Willy's sister up on Hyde Park Road."

Putting police business aside for a moment, Roybal said, "Known him a long time, haven't you?"

"Twenty years," Patch replied, then paused. "We got to hangin' out when we were both students at the Indian school. I sort of looked out after him. Been friends ever since."

Then Patch went quiet, looking at the ground—relishing the memory.

"We'll get 'em for you. We'll find out who did this."

Roybal's sense of real humanity, rarely shown, was leaking out.

"I just hope Willy can hang in there 'til then," Patch said, releasing a big sigh.

He nodded to Roybal and headed back down the alley, leaving the cop to do his job.

At St. Vincent's Hospital, Patch found Willy laying unconscious in bed hooked up to a variety of machines. A nurse busily tended to his partner and the machines. A doctor was just leaving Willy's room.

"Doc, how's he doing?" Patch asked.

"It's touch and go at this point," he said shaking his head. "He took two bullets at close range, but luckily they missed his heart."

The busy doctor pushed on to the next patient waiting for his care.

The sounds of the heart monitor and the respirator pounded in Patch's head. He stared helplessly at his old friend. Why'd it have to be Willy, Patch thought. He'd never hurt a soul in his life.

"Hang in there, buddy," Patch whispered out loud. "I'll get to the bottom of this thing."

There was nothing he could do for his friend there, so he left. He needed time to think.

Outside the hospital, Patch caught a cab, telling the driver to take him out to the National Cemetery on the north edge of town. The white rows of meticulously placed head stones marked the end of the trail for hundreds of military veterans. Patch's father was one of them.

After paying the cabby, the P.I. jumped the low fence surrounding the cemetery and marched toward his father's grave. It had been quite awhile since Patch had paid his dad a visit. He used to come out regularly to have little talks, something that rarely happened when his father was alive.

Patch located the stone: 39th row, 23rd from the end. Sgt. Anderson Victorio Geronimo, served in Vietnam 1968-69. Wounded in action while leading a seige against an enemy bunker. Received the Purple Heart. Died in 1999 after a long bout with alcoholism and diabetes.

A visit to this site always gave Patch time to reflect on his own personal history. It might be hard for someone to understand how a person could come to be named John J. Geronimo. You had to know the family tree.

Patch's father's father was a white man named Winslow Homer Jones. He came to the Mescalero reservation as an employee of the BIA to head up the tribe's reservation police force. Once there, the Welch immigrant met Patch's Apache grandmother, Sonsee-array, Morning Star, descendant of the original Geronimo. The couple was married in a traditional tribal ceremony and blessed with three children. Smallpox took two of the kids, leaving Patch's father as the only survivor.

At age eighteen Anderson Victorio Geronimo married his fullblood childhood sweetheart, Ela Ortega. After serving a tour in Nam, he returned to the rez to become a tribal cop like his father. John Jones Geronimo was the couple's first born of four kids, deciding to rearrange the last and middle names. The tragedies befalling the Jones family in later years were what shaped—or maybe misshaped is a better word—the man now standing in the Santa Fe cemetery in the middle of the night.

Patch reached in his pocket and took out his pouch of tobacco. He reverently placed the offering to his father's spirit on the simple tombstone.

Patch found, however, that he didn't have much to say to his father's spirit tonight. The feelings and the words were all choked up inside, as usual. He'd mostly quit making these graveside pilgrimages when he realized that he had turned out more like his father than he wanted to admit. Anyway, what had begun as attempted self-therapy sessions had degenerated into angry tirades against his father's shortcomings, failures and weaknesses. So Patch had quit coming.

Why he'd come tonight wasn't clear.

"It wasn't all your fault," Patch admitted out loud, and then he turned to walk home.

Half an hour later, he entered his apartment and turned on the light. Tossing his jacket over the back of a chair, he headed for the kitchenette.

Seeing Willy in the hospital had reminded Patch of his own pain. Like so many other Native people, he had a wounded and troubled soul. The sources of this pain are rooted in history and human psychology. But seldom did he reveal this pain to anyone. And he never showed his internal scars. He just stuffed the feelings and moved on. Self-medication was the go-to solution.

He took the glass out of the sink and removed the bottle of gin from the cabinet. Opening the built-in refrigerator, he took out a bottle of tonic water. He poured both the gin and the tonic in the glass at the same time and quickly downed the drink. He poured another.

With glass in hand, he took out his phone and punched in a familiar number on the pad. While the phone rang, he downed the second drink. As he set the glass down on the night stand, he noticed the time: 4:30 am.

Jessie's sleepy voice came on the phone.

"Sorry to wake you," Patch said. "It's me."

He took a deep breath.

"Willy's been shot. In an alley off Old Santa Fe Trail. That's all I know about it so far. He's in intensive care."

Patch allowed the news to sink in for a moment.

"I need you to do something for me," he continued. After a moment's hesitation to build up some courage, he asked, "Will you go over to Rachel's and tell her? I just can't do it."

"What?" Jessie exclaimed. "Left your balls in your purse, did you?"

Patch knew he had that coming, but he didn't want to give Jessie the satisfaction of acknowledging it.

"Have her come to the office around ten in the morning," he said. "I'll talk to her then. Thanks, Jess, you're the best."

Not waiting for a response, he clicked off the call and went to the closet. Rummaging around for a minute, he pulled out an old cardboard box full of odds and ends. He came up with the pearl-handled Colt .45 he kept in there. It had been a gift from his father, passed down from his grandfather, Winslow, an old style lawman if there ever was one.

He was sitting on the edge of the bed admiring the pistol when the front doorbell buzzed.

Startled, Patch looked towards the door. "Who is it?" he said with obvious irritation.

"Patch, it's Sam. We've got to talk to you."

"Just a minute," Patch responded with more irritation.

He hurried to put the box back in the closet and cover it up.

"Who's we?" he asked as he opened the front door.

Standing outside with Roybal was an Anglo man dressed in a suit and overcoat. Patch had noticed him with Roybal at the alley crime scene, but hadn't paid him much attention. He was a large, barrel-chested man in his mid-50s, chewing on a cigarillo.

"This is our new Chief of Detectives," Roybal offered. "Lieutenant Frank Johnson."

Patch tried to conceal his irritation.

"Hello, Lieutenant. Is this a social call at four-thirty in the morning?" Patch knew it wasn't.

Ignoring his question, Johnson said, "We'd like a word with you, if we may."

Patch responded with a feigned friendly manner, "Sure, sure. Come on in, gents. Mi casa, su casa."

The two men entered. Patch closed the door behind them as they headed for the sofa. Roybal and Johnson sat down on the cloth-covered couch while Patch headed for the kitchenette. He poured himself another drink. He downed it and turned toward the men.

"Well, what'll it be, gents?" he asked cheerily. "Coffee or whiskey?"

The men simultaneously answered.

"Whiskey," Roybal said.

"Coffee," Johnson said.

Johnson glared at Roybal. Roybal changed his mind.

"Nothing for us, thanks." Johnson spoke for both of them. "We'll take a rain-check." Roybal was disappointed.

"Suit yourselves," Patch said. He was already tired of their company, and he was pretty sure that this wasn't going to be pleasant, whatever it was they had to say.

He put the bottle down on the kitchen cabinet and looked at it longingly for a second. Leaving it, Patch sat down in a chair opposite the pair of policemen.

"Did you break the news to Willy's sister?" Roybal started. "What's her name?"

"Rachel," Patch said. "Yes, I did."

"How'd she take it?" Roybal continued.

"Hard," Patch said, rather annoyed. "How'd you expect her to take it?"

Johnson leaned toward Patch, dropping all pretense of cordiality. "What kind of gun do you carry, Geronimo?" he asked.

"I don't," Patch responded coolly. "Don't like them, don't need one. There's a couple at the office, though."

"You keep one here?" Johnson pried.

"Nope," Patch said, still cool. Unconsciously, he cut his eyes toward the closet, then back to the men. "You can take a look if you like. It don't matter to me."

Patch's face hardened, and he leaned toward Johnson. "As long as you got a warrant."

Roybal shifted in his seat nervously. "We're not accusing you of anything, Patch," he said.

Patch didn't take his eyes off Johnson. "What are you guys fishing for?" he demanded. "Get to it or get out," he said as he stood up.

"Don't be that way, Patch," Roybal pleaded. "We're only doing our job."

Johnson stood up and confronted Patch face to face. "Why were you tailing Morgan?" he asked.

"I wasn't," Patch said firmly. "Willy was, because a client paid us good money to tail him. And look what he got for it."

"So who's the client?" Johnson asked dryly.

"You know I don't have to tell you that," Patch snapped.

"You've got to help us out here, Patch," Roybal interrupted politely. "How can we find out who shot Willy if you won't tell us what you know?"

"We know you didn't go to Willy's sister's house," Johnson said bluntly. "What did you do, have your secretary tell her?"

Lucky guess, Patch thought. His face remained unreadable.

"That would give you plenty of time to get to Morgan's place," Johnson continued.

"What's this Anglo talking about?" Patch asked Roybal sarcastically.

"Murder, Mr. Geronimo," Johnson answered. "Murder. Morgan was shot down in front of his hotel about half an hour after you left the alley."

Patch moved away and waved his hand in front of his face. "What did you have for dinner last night, Lieutenant?

"What time did you get home?" he asked, ignoring Patch's remark.

Patch reached for his papers and tobacco, and began rolling a cigarette. "I went by the hospital to see Willy," he said. "Then I walked around for awhile, thinking things over. I came here, poured myself a couple of drinks, then you two showed up."

"Where'd you walk to?" Johnson asked.

"No place in particular," Patch replied.

"Anybody see you?" Johnson continued.

"I don't think so," Patch responded. "Maybe a ghost or two."

Then Patch realized where this line of questioning was going. "No, there were no witnesses. None that could talk anyway."

Patch chuckled.

"What's so funny?" Johnson said.

"Nothing," Patch said, walking back to the kitchenette.

"Sit down, Lieutenant," he said calmly. "Are you sure you won't have a drink?"

"Yeah, I'm sure," he said. Johnson sat down.

Patch relaxed and poured himself another drink. Walking over to the bed, he sat down on the edge.

"Now I understand where you guys are coming from," he told them. "Sorry to get all riled up. It's been a helluva night. Sam here will tell you. I've always tried to watch out for Willy. He's like a brother to me. So you can imagine how upsetting this whole thing is. So how did Morgan get it?"

"Four times in the back with a forty-five," Johnson answered matter-of-factly. "And you know how it is around here. Nobody saw nothing. Nobody heard nothing."

"Anybody at the hotel know anything about him?" Patch liked asking the questions.

"Only that he'd been here a week," Roybal volunteered.

"Anybody with him?" Patch kept pressing.

"No," Roybal said, obligingly. "He was alone."

Johnson broke the flow.

"We were planning on asking you these questions, hoping you had some answers. Like, who was this guy? What was he up to?"

"I never laid eyes on Morgan, dead or alive," Patch explained.

Johnson stood up and motioned to Roybal that it was time to leave. They walked toward the door as Patch followed.

Stopping at the door, Johnson turned to Patch.

"Roybal here has filled me in on you," he said. "Says you're a straight shooter. You'll get a square deal from me, John, whether you did it or not. Can't really blame you if you did. Sorry about your partner and all, but I'd still have to nail you if you did Morgan in."

"Of course you would," Patch said. "I wouldn't expect anything different."

Johnson shook his hand and they said goodnight all friendly and chummy-like.

Patch walked over and stood by the edge of the bed. As he started to undress, he said to himself, "so that's how it's going to be."

3 **Chapter Three**

Morning often had a rude way of intruding itself, bright and cheery, into your life when you least wanted it. At least that's the way Patch felt about it today.

He had dragged his tired body to the office around 9:30 a.m. and was gazing out his office window from the comfort of his leather chair. The Plaza was coming to life with tourists and opening shops. But he wasn't focused on anything so immediate as the Plaza or the downtown rooftops. As he rolled a cigarette, his mind replayed a scene from his childhood on the Mescalero Reservation.

It was a 4th of July weekend when the tribe held its annual Coming of Age ceremonies for girls who were entering puberty. Hundreds of Apaches from all over the country returned to the rez for the four day festivities. His Uncle Wasco had come in from Oklahoma for the occasion and was camping next to Patch and his family who lived in the nearby, off-reservation town of Alamagordo.

Patch was ten years old at the time and still a little frightened of the mysterious and dramatic Crown Dancers who ended the ceremony each night. Patch had vaguely known that these were really men dressed up to impersonate the Spirits of the

Mountain Gods, but that didn't diminish their power in the young boy's mind.

It was a Saturday night and the Crown Dancers were in full swing around the central bonfire at the ceremonial grounds. Patch, however, was hanging out with Uncle Wasco back at the camp while every one else enjoyed the dancing. Uncle Wasco was well on his way to complete intoxication, which was against the tribe's strict rules for the event. Alcoholic beverages were forbidden on the dance grounds, which is why Wasco did all his drinking in his tent.

"Why don't you have a little drink with me, Geronimo?" his uncle said as the boy read a comic book. "It'll make a man out of you."

"I don't think I'm supposed to," the boy replied. "I don't think you're supposed to either."

"Oh, you can't go through life always doin' what your supposed to," the drunk said. "We're Apaches. We don't have to follow the rules everybody else does."

He opened a can of beer and held it out for his nephew.

"Besides, I'm your uncle. I'm supposed to teach you about being Apache. Real Apaches aren't afraid of nothing."

"I'm not afraid."

"Well, go on then. Prove it."

Patch studied the can his uncle dangled in front of him. Suddenly he grabbed the can and took a drink. It tasted awful, and his face showed it. Wasco laughed.

"Aw, go on," Wasco coaxed. "A real Apache wouldn't let a little bad taste stop him. But I guess, if you aren't a real–."

Patch began guzzling the foul tasting stuff before his uncle could say the word "Apache" another time. When the boy finished off the first one, his uncle dared him to drink another. And down that one went, too.

They were so engrossed in their little illicit activity, they hadn't heard Patch's father approaching the tent. All of a sudden the flap flew open, and in stepped Anderson. When he saw the beer in his son's hand, he slapped the boy hard across the face. The beer and the boy went flying across the tent.

What happened next had remained a blur in Patch's mind to this day. His father lunged at Wasco, pushing the drunk through the canvass. The tent collapsed around Patch. He heard the terrible sounds of a violent fight going on outside as he struggled to find an opening. His cheek throbbed with pain.

By the time he found his way out of the folds of the fallen tent, the fight was over. His father was standing over his uncle's bloody body. Two tribal policemen arrived on the scene just as Patch realized that his uncle was somehow dead.

"Get him to the hospital," his father, the tribal cop, commanded the other two. "He assaulted me and was contributing to the delenquency of a minor."

Patch watched as his father escorted his uncle's body away. No one in his family ever spoke of that night again.

That's about the time the dream, the nightmare, had begun. In the dream, Patch was holding that can of beer. He could hear the eerie warbles and whoops of the Mountain Spirit Dancers in the distance. All of a sudden, the four frightful ceremonial dancers were surrounding him. They smeared the black paint from their bodies on his face. Their black, lifeless eyes stared into his soul. He knew they tormented him because he drank the beer. His dead uncle cackled a hideous laughter somewhere behind them.

He used to always wake up in a panicked sweat. Patch stopped having the dream when he went off to college and decided that Indian religion was no more than quaint superstition. But the drinking was yet to end. It was now Patch's religion.

The sound of his office door opening brought Patch back to the present.

"Yes, Jessie?" he said without turning around.

Jessie entered the room and closed the door behind her. "She's out there," the secretary said in a low flirtatious tone. "Rachel's waiting for you to go and comfort her."

Patch swiveled his chair around.

"Give it a rest, Jessie," he scolded. "This is no time to be a smart ass."

She dropped the attitude.

"Sorry. I'll send her in," Jessie said.

"Good girl," Patch nodded. He finished rolling his cigarette as Rachel entered.

Rachel was the kind of woman that made a man's jaw drop: a beautiful American Indian woman in her mid-30's with long raven-black hair and full lips. Nothing about her told you that she was Willy's sister.

As she entered Patch's office, he noticed that her eyes were puffy and red from crying. She clutched a kleenex tightly in her hand.

"Hi, Rachel," Patch said tenderly, moving to her from behind his desk. "Hell of a deal, ain't it?"

"Oh, Patch," she sobbed as they embraced in the middle of the room. He touched her cheek to comfort her and began to kiss her. She submitted and kissed him back for a moment. Suddenly she stopped and pushed him away.

"No you don't, you son of a bitch," she said angrily.

"No I don't, what?" he asked with a puzzled look.

Rachel moved back a step. "Don't play dumb with me," she reprimanded.

"I ain't playin," he replied. "What's going on?"

"Willy's laying up in that hospital with a hole in his chest and you want to know what's going on?"

She paced.

"What was it this time, Patch? Some angry husband out gunning for you and he got Willy instead?"

She was getting angrier by the minute. "Did you send Willy out last night to save your own ass?" Now she was yelling. "Did you set Willy up, Patch?"

"You know I didn"t," he yelled back. "Why would you even say such a damn thing?"

She broke into tears.

"Then why was he out there in a dark alley all alone in the middle of the night? You were supposed to take care of him. You promised me you'd take care of him."

She was sobbing.

Her words hit Patch like heavy blows. He walked to the window and gazed out at the street below.

"Don't you think I know that?" he said finally. "Don't you think that's all I've thought about ever since I got the call last night? It was a set-up all right, and I am probably the one who was supposed to take the bullet, not Willy."

He dropped into his leather chair with a sigh. Rachel, sobered by his words, began to regain her composure.

"We both know that Willy doesn't approve of our relationship," Patch said softly.

Then anger overtook him.

"But you got a lot of nerve saying I had anything to do with Willy getting hurt."

He paused and calmed down.

"Go home. Get some rest. Get your mind uncluttered, Rachel."

He turned back to the window and motioned for her to leave.

"All right, Patch," she said as she stood up. "I'm going to the hospital. I'll call you later."

"Yeah, whatever," Patch said dismissively.

Rachel exited his office, leaving the door ajar. Shortly, Jessie stepped in.

"What was that all about?" she asked.

"She thinks I set Willy up," Patch replied.

Jessie came over to the desk and sat on the edge near Patch.

"Where'd she get a weird idea like that?" she said.

"Beats me." That's all Patch could say.

She opened his desk drawer and pulled out the tobacco bag and the rolling papers he kept there and began rolling a cigarette.

"She thinks I got Willy shot," Patch said sourly. "The police think I murdered Morgan. What about you? What do you think?"

She finished rolling the cigarette and licked it suggestively with her tongue. Then she smoothed it out and put it in Patch's mouth.

"I think you're in over your head," she said as she fumbled around in his desk drawer for a cigarette lighter. "And I think there's more to this Barkley woman than she let on. That's what I think."

She came up with a lighter and lit his cigarette.

"Why are you so good to me, Jessie?" Patch asked sweetly. "I don't deserve it."

He put an arm around her waist and rested his cheek against her hip.

"I know you don't," she quipped, as she removed his arm from her waist and stepped away from the desk.

"But what I want to know is what's it going to take to get Rachel out of your system?" she continued. "You know it's a dead end."

"Yeah, it is," he replied with a certain resignation. "She's too comfortable in that big house her husband bought her. But I don't know how to end it."

"You'll only be able to end it when you realize that you have no power over it," she said.

"What?" He stared at her blankly.

It's one of your addictions, like the booze. The first step in ridding your life of any addiction is recognizing that your powerless to control it."

"What's this?" Patch asked, "A. A. lecture number thirty seven?"

She stepped closer to him.

"Look at me, Patch," Jessie demanded. Obediently, but reluctantly, he looked at her.

"You've always gotten by on your good looks, your good luck and your charm," she chided. "But it's gonna catch up to you. It's already caught up to Willy, and he was just an innocent bystander."

Mocking her, Patch wagged his finger in her face while wagging his head from side to side. Just then, the phone on Patch's desk rang. Jessie picked it up, still looking at Patch with a certain amount of disgust.

"Eagle Eye Investigations," she said into the phone. "Just a moment."

She covered the mouthpiece and whispered "It's for you. The mysterious Ms. Barkley."

Patch took the phone.

"Ms. Barkley. I was wondering if I'd hear from you again. Oh, yeah? Okay, wait a minute." He motioned to Jessie to write something down. She picked up a pencil and pad.

"What's that address?" he asked into the phone. "Pinon Apartments, 213 West Galesteo, Apartment D. All right, I'll be there in a few minutes."

He hung up the phone and rose from his seat. Retrieving the piece of note paper from Jessie, he gave her a little kiss on the cheek.

"Gotta go, babe," he told her. "Ms. Barkley has some 'splainin' to do," he said in his best Ricky Ricardo impersonation.

"Be careful," Jessie said sincerely. "Something's not right with that woman."

Patch smiled and winked.

"Anything for you, doll."

She winced at the word "doll."

"You know I hate it when you call me that. It's so… chauvinistic!"

"I know. That's why I say it."

His sarcastic smile dissolved into a look of grim determination as he turned and left the office.

Jessie absent-mindedly rubbed the spot on her cheek where Patch had kissed her. She gazed out the window as a whimsical little smile came to her face. She hoped he never realized what a crush she had on that man. He was just her type, the type to use you, then discard you.

Patch arrived at Ms. Barkley's pink adobe apartment complex a few minutes later. He found her door and rang the buzzer. She quickly opened the ornately carved Spanish colonial door. Her face was flushed and her hair somewhat tousled. She wore sweat pants and a tight fitting t-shirt.

"Come in, Mr. Geronimo," she said.

Patch entered, and she closed the door, leaning back against it for a moment. Cardboard boxes and suitcases were scattered around the front room of her apartment.

"Please excuse the mess," she said. "I haven't finished unpacking."

She removed a half-empty box from a nearby chair and motioned for Patch to sit down. She sat on one of the unpacked boxes nearby.

"Mr. Geronimo, I have a confession to make," she offered. "That story I told you yesterday was all... was just..."

"Was just a story," he said. "Is that what you're trying to say, Ms—just what is your name, anyway?"

"Sykes," she responded. "Kathleen Sykes."

"Well, Ms. Sykes," Patch began, "It wasn't your story that actually convinced us to do your dirty work for you. It was your three hundred dollars."

"So you blame me for what happened to your partner," she said remorsefully.

"Let's put it this way," he said with a hard edge. "He wouldn't be up there in that hospital ward hooked up to a dozen machines with half the hospital staff swarming around him if you hadn't come in with your sob story yesterday." Then he softened his tone. "But, no, I don't blame you, not exactly."

She stood up and began pacing nervously around the room.

"If it makes you feel any better, I am sorry for what happened," she said. "I didn't for a minute expect anyone to get hurt." She peaked out the window through the blinds.

"That's all water under the bridge," Patch explained. "But there's a whole herd of policemen and a courtroom full of D.A.s out there trying to put the puzzle pieces together, and some of them are pointing fingers at me. So why don't we cut the crap and get down to the business at hand?"

"Do they know about me?" the blonde asked.

"Not yet," Patch replied. "I've claimed client confidentiality for the time being."

"I'd like to keep it that way," she said. "Is that possible?"

"That all depends on what you have to say to me in the next few minutes," Patch said with a fake smile. Dropping the smile, he added, "And it better be good."

"I can't tell you too much," she started. "Not yet. You've got to trust me, Geronimo."

Then she turned on what passed for charm where she's from.

"I'm all alone and afraid. I need your help. I can tell you're a brave man, strong and confident. Certainly you can spare a little for me."

With a dramatic flare, she dropped herself on the floor at Patch's feet and clutched his hand.

"Help me, Geronimo," she pleaded. "I know I don't have the right to ask, but please help me."

Her eyes beckoned to him. Patch was unmoved.

"You think you're pretty good, don't you?" he said staring straight at her. "It's those eyes, and the way you pout that pretty little lower lip. Yeah, you're a real pro."

She jumped to her feet, her eyes flaring with rage. Realizing that wouldn't get her anywhere, she cooled down.

"Okay, I deserved that," she said finally. "But I'm not lying."

"You're not lying now, or you weren't lying then?" Patch asked coldly.

"I don't blame you for being so cold," she said.

Patch gave it to her straight.

"Lady, hanging around you can be hazardous to one's health. We could all be lying in that hospital room in a coma before it's all over because of you. Now, out with it or I'm going to the police about you. You can start with Morgan. Who is he, and what is he to you?"

"Morgan and I were supposed to be partners."

She paced as she spoke.

"We both used to work for a man named Coulter, Ryan Coulter. He's sort of an art dealer. He has offices in San Francisco and New York. I worked out of the Frisco office. Anyway, he sent me and Morgan here to Santa Fe to open another office for him."

"But you were suspicious of Morgan, is that it?" Patch asked. "So you wanted him followed?"

"That's right."

Kathleen was glad he seemed to understand.

"I had to know what he was up to, to see if I could trust him."

"I guess so, since you two were gonna cut in on your boss's action," Patch said unsympathetically. "Must be a lot of money in art these days. Was it Coulter who hit Morgan?"

"I'm sure of it," Kathleen replied. "You're good at reading between the lines."

"Occupational hazard," Patch said. "Comes from working for suspicious wives and disgruntled husbands. But go on with your story."

"That's all I can really tell you now," Kathleen concluded. "Except to say that I am in danger, and I do need your help."

40

"All right then," Patch said. "But I'll need more information soon and some funds to operate on if you want me to keep you safe."

"How much?" she asked.

"Five hundred for now," he replied.

"All right," she agreed. "I'll get it from the bedroom."

While she was out of the room, Patch decided to snoop around a little. He opened one of the boxes, finding a stack of books on American Indian art and artifacts. He pulled out a book titled <u>Tribal Treasures From The Southwest</u>. A yellow piece of paper, acting as a bookmark, protruded from the top of the book. Hearing footsteps, he quickly dropped the book back into the box.

Kathleen came into the living room holding five one-hundred dollar bills. As she extended her hand to give him the money, Patch grabbed her arm and pulled her close to him.

"Stay inside and don't open the door for anyone but me," Patch said forcefully. "I'll be back, hopefully with good news."

He looked deep into her eyes for a moment, then kissed her on the mouth. She kissed him back, hard. Then he took the bills from her hand and turned to leave. Kathleen stood transfixed as the door closed behind him.

In a few minutes, Patch was walking across the Plaza once again. As usual, an odd assortment of tourists ambled in every direction. Patch glanced up at his office, then down at the La Fonda Hotel which was just across Old Santa Fe Trail. He quickly crossed the street against the light and took the few steps up to the hotel door.

Crossing the polished tile floor, he headed for the front desk to speak to the hotel clerk. An Indian man was at the desk.

"Seen Jackson lately?" Patch asked him.

The clerk pointed across the lobby, indicating a man seated on a bench reading a newspaper that completely concealed him. Patch walked over to the bench and sat down.

"You hotel detectives are a hard working lot," Patch said dryly.

Jackson dropped the newspaper and, seeing Patch, smiled. Jackson Hightower, an Anglo man in his mid-50s, was wearing his version of "tourist clothes" to help him blend in.

"You know me," Jackson said. "I follow the path of least resistance. Sorry to hear about Willy."

"Thanks," Patch said. "Listen, what can you tell me about this fellow Morgan? He was supposedly a guest here. Willy was following him when he got shot."

"I can tell you what I told the cops," Jackson replied. "Walk with me. I'm gonna get a cappuccino or something."

The two men walked down a hallway toward the back of the hotel. Jackson talked as they walked.

"I'd seen him hanging around the hotel for about a week. Him and that blonde bombshell. I really couldn't tell what they were up to. The night Willy was shot I was on duty. Willy showed up about 7:45. He told me he was on a case and to ignore him for the rest of the night. So about eight, the blonde shows up. Then Morgan comes in. After a few minutes, they part company. Willy tails Morgan. Then the blonde returns. Now I'm curious. She calls somebody on the lobby pay phone. The conversation heats up. She gets mad and slams the phone down."

Patch and Jackson stopped a few feet from an espresso cart parked at the end of the hallway near a side entrance to the hotel. There were a couple of people already waiting in line.

"Now here's what I didn't tell the cops," Jackson continued. "There was one thing she said on the phone that I caught clearly.

42

She said I need you here. The situation's getting out of my control."

The line at the espresso counter cleared and they walked the remaining few steps to the counter.

Patch's curiosity was definitely aroused.

"The situation's getting out of my control," he repeated. "Why didn't you tell this to the police?"

"Cause I was saving it for you," he said with a smile.

"Thanks," Patch replied. "I need anything and everything I can get to point the cops in the right direction. Keep your eyes open, okay?"

"Sure thing, Patch," Jackson said.

Patch pulled a few one dollar bills out of his pants pocket and placed them on the espresso counter.

"Get him whatever he wants," Patch said to the server. "I gotta run, pal. See ya later."

Jackson nodded and Patch exited the hotel by the back side door. He crossed the street to his office.

To reach Patch's office, you could also enter a short back alleyway behind the building and mount an old set of stairs up to the second floor. It was part of the charm of officing in historic downtown Santa Fe.

As Patch mounted those stairs, his mind was working a mile a minute, trying to make what few clues he had fit together. But it was just too early in the game.

As he entered the office, he found Jessie doing some hand-work, sewing a Native American bead design on a leather pouch. She was about to speak when the phone rang.

"Eagle Eye Investigations," Jessie answered. "I'm sorry, sir. You'll have to speak up. Your voice is muffled." She listened intently. "Yes, he's here. Just a moment, please."   She covered the mouthpiece and whispered to Patch.

"Sounds like a weirdo. He has a strange sounding voice."

As Patch took the phone from Jessie, he noticed her beadwork and smiled at her.

"This is Geronimo," he said into the phone. "What can I do for you?"

"I have some information about the party who shot your partner," the muffled voice said.

The smile left Patch's face. He reached across Jessie's desk and turned on a digital recorder that allowed him to record the conversation.

"Who's this?" he asked.

"A perfect stranger," the voice answered. "Meet me at the Cross of the Martyrs tonight at nine p.m. I'll tell you more then."

"How will I know you?" Patch asked, but the phone went dead. Patch looked at the receiver, then replaced it on the hook. He turned off the digital recorder.

"Copy that audio file onto a thumb drive for me, Jessie," Patch told her. "I may need to let Roybal hear it later." Jessie dug around in her desk drawer for a thumb drive as Patch headed for the door.

"Hold down the camp for me, honey," he said just before leaving. "I've got to see Ms. Barkley again. She's got some more 'splainin' to do."

He went out the door without seeing the twinge of jealousy in Jessie's eyes.

Minutes later, Kathleen was pleasantly surprised to see Patch standing outside her front door as she peered through the peep hole. Wearing only a bath robe this time, she wrapped a towel around her wet hair and opened the door.

"Back so soon?" she said. "Good news, I hope."

Patch pushed past her into the apartment. "Maybe not," he said coolly. "It's time for a game of truth or consequences. I'll be Drew Carey."

Ignoring his attitude, she moved close to him and pushed him down on to the couch. She sat down beside him, her body touching his. She looked straight into his eyes.

"Okay, what do you want to know?" she asked.

"Who else is working with you, for starters," he barked.

"I have a silent partner," she admitted.

"Me, too," Patch interjected.

"He's a financial backer, she continued. "Acquiring Indian art objects isn't cheap you know."

"What's his name?" Patch barked again.

"I can't tell you," she said. "That's part of the deal. He wants to remain anonymous."

Patch opened his mouth to ask another question, but the blonde gave him an open-mouth kiss before he could speak. She began removing his jacket. Her phone began ringing, but she ignored it.

Pulling away from her, Patch said, "You'd better answer that. It might be your silent partner."

As she stood up, the front of her robe fell open revealing a tantalizing portion of her naked body. She delayed a moment before covering herself. Patch noticed.

She picked up the cordless phone and said, "Yes?" She listened for a moment and frowned a little. "This isn't a good time. Can you call back later?" Patch watched her closely, looking for any clues about the caller.

"Yes, I have the information ready," Kathleen continued, "But it's not convenient to go over it now."

Unhappy with how the conversation was going, she rolled her eyes for Patch's benefit.

"All right, all right," she said. "But I'll have to go into the other room and get my notes. Hang on."

She held the phone to her chest. "Business," she said to Patch apologetically. "Don't go away. I'll be right back."

She dashed into the bedroom.

Meanwhile Patch took the opportunity to scan the room. He noticed that a few more boxes had been put away since his last visit. He managed to find the box of books he was looking at the last time. Reaching inside, he located the <u>Tribal Treasures of the Southwest</u> book again. It still had the yellow paper book mark inside. This time he noticed the book's cover read "Volume 24" under the title.

Thumbing through it, he saw photos of Hopi Katchinas, Navajo Sandpaintings and Pueblo fetish carvings. Under each photo, there were prices, collectors' names and museum listings. These weren't exactly what Patch would call Indian art. They were more like sacred artifacts—religious objects probably stolen from the original tribal owners.

He turned to the page where the yellow bookmark was, finding a photo of a pair of rather plain, carved wooden statues. "Zuni War Gods," the caption read. He made a mental note of the items and the page number, then replaced the book in its box. Growing impatient, he looked around the room once more, then quietly let himself out the front door.

On his way back to the office, he stopped into the New Mexico State Historical Library located in the back of the Palace of the Governors. Stepping in from the street, he had to allow his eyes time to adjust to the dimly lit old room. It smelled of musty books and four-hundred-year old antiquated ideas.

"Geronimo, is that you?" a familiar voice rang out loudly, almost shaking the dust from the rafters. An old Hispanic man with white hair and mustache approached Patch from a back room. His glasses were pulled up on his forehead. He squinted at Patch.

"Pedro, you old Spaniard. Read any good books lately?"

Pedro laughed.

"Now I know it's you," he said. "You haven't greeted me any other way in the ten years I've known you."

He grabbed Patch and hugged him robustly.

"How the hell are you?" he asked his much younger friend.

"I've been better, Pedro," Patch confessed. "Did you hear about Willy?"

"Of course, my friend. People are talking about it all over town. How is he doing?"

"Too early to tell, Pedro, but that's why I'm here. I'm trying to find out who did it, and I need your help."

"Anything I can do, just name it."

"There's a book, or really a series of books, <u>Tribal Treasures of the Southwest</u>. Do you know it?"

"Yes, I think I do. It's some sort of listing of American Indian artifacts, I believe."

"Do you have a copy?" Patch asked. "I need volume twenty-four."

"Let's see," the old man replied. He went to the card catalog and began flipping through the brittle, yellowed cards.

"Tribal Treasures, Tribal Treasures—Ah, here it is."

He pulled out the card and headed for a book shelf. Patch followed.

"They publish a new volume every year with the latest prices on museum-quality pieces," he said as he walked.

When Pedro reached the shelf he was looking for, he scanned the spines of the books with his finger. His finger stopped on an empty space where the book should have been.

"Oh, I forgot. The current volume, volume twenty four, is out on a three day loan. It'll be back tomorrow."

"What about an earlier volume?" Patch asked.

"It's sort of an odd subscription thing with the publisher. We get a new issue each year and return the old one to them. It's the bible of Indian art and artifact sales business. Is it important?"

"I don't know yet. It's part of the puzzle that may lead to Willy's shooter."

"Well, then, I'll make sure it's returned first thing in the morning. You can call for it by ten o'clock."

"Thanks, Pedro. I appreciate your help."

That night Patch made sure he was at the Cross of the Martyrs a little early. For about a half an hour he paced back and forth on the hill. Be begin to loose patience.

He looked at his watch. It read 9:15. Patch figured the guy was a no-show. He threw down his almost-finished cigarette, crushed it under foot and turned to leave. Then he noticed a dark car in the nearby parking lot flashing its headlights. Patch headed towards the car when, out of nowhere, a group of five older teenage boys holding skateboards approached and encircled him.

They moved towards Patch threateningly, forcing him toward the paved path which zig-zagged down the hill to the street below. Once on the path, the skateboarders mounted their boards and began herding Patch down the path. They careened past him one after the other, taunting him and keeping him off balance.

Patch realized that he could easily push them off their boards or shove them into the retaining wall as they passed, and he did. After a couple of them took a dive, a signal from the group

48

leader brought out switch-blades from everyone in the group. They proceeded to swing blades at Patch as they skated past him. Working his way down the path, he managed to evade their blades, and eventually he reached the bottom of the hill. There, automobile and pedestrian traffic made it too risky for the skateboarders to continue their campaign of harrasment so they dispersed.

After they had disappeared, Patch checked himself over, straightened his clothing and found a couple of slits where knife blades came too close. He walked the three blocks home.

He entered his apartment, turned on the light and was startled by Rachel who was sitting on the couch with a drink in her hand. She was wearing a semi-formal, low-cut dress. Her handbag, diamond earrings and high heels were on the coffee table. Patch was very surprised to see her there.

"Rachel, what are you doing here?"

"I was beginning to wonder about you," she said with a slight slur. "Thought maybe you had another girlfriend on the side."

Then she noticed his ripped clothing. Alarmed, she rushed to him, opening his jacket.

"What happened," she asked, sounding a bit more sober. "Are you hurt?"

"I'm just fine,' Patch assured her as he removed his jacket. "Somebody was playing a little joke. Thought they'd scare me off the case."

He poured himself a drink from the bottle on the kitchenette counter.

"Where's Walter tonight?"

"Oh, he's at some gallery owner's meeting. They're worried about Indian Market this year."

She began unbuttoning his shirt.

"Listen, about this morning," she continued. "I'm sorry for the way I acted. I was upset. I didn't know what I was saying."

"It's okay," Patch said, pulling away from her. "Forget it. I've been wanting to talk to you. About us."

Rachel reached up and put her forefinger on his lips to shush him. A tear formed in the corner of her eye.

"Not now, Patch, please," she said. "I need you. Especially tonight."

Patch wiped the tear from her eye and kissed her tenderly. He picked her up and carried her to the bed. He pulled his shirt off, sat down on the edge of the bed to remove his shoes. With one shoe still in his hand, Rachel pulled him down to her and they kissed deeply.

4 Chapter Four

Next morning, Patch left Rachel asleep in his bed. When he got to the office, Jessie was reading the morning paper.

"What's the latest, Jessie dear?" he asked as he closed the front office door.

"Antique tribal art collectors gather for Indian Market," she said, quoting the front page headline.

"Does that mean that the collectors are antiques or that the art is antique?" Patch asked.

"Ha, ha," Jessie replied sarcastically. Putting the paper down, she looked up at him.

"So, anything come "up" at Ms. Barkley's yesterday?"

"Ha, ha, back at you, Jessie," Patch snapped. "Sarcasm doesn't become you at all. What's stirring here?"

"The joint's jumping already today," she said, dropping the attitude. "An elderly Indian man came in to see you earlier, and a mister—.

She stopped to examine a business card sitting on her desk.

"Mr. Kyoto, a Japanese man."

She handed him the card. There was a lizard logo on the card along with his name and a San Francisco address.

"He wants you to meet him at the Thunderbird for coffee," she said. "He's there now."

"Who was the Native man?" Patch asked.

"He didn't leave his name," she said. "Just said he'd stop by again later."

Changing the subject, Patch said, "Okay, listen, I've got a job for you."

He fished around in his pocket, came up with a piece of paper and handed it to her.

"While I meet with Kyoto," he continued, "Could you go over to the history library and pick up this book? Old Mr. Santero is suppose to have it for me this morning. I think it'll help us get a line on what our Ms. Barkley is up to. Drop it off at my place, then go check on Willy and take the rest of the day off."

"Cool," Jessie replied. She grabbed her purse and jacket, and they exited the office together. At the bottom of the stairs they went their separate ways.

Patch headed down the street toward the Thunderbird Bar and Grill. After climbing the stairs that took you to the second story restaurant, he told the hostess he was looking for an oriental man already dining there. She led him to the only oriental in the place, seated on the balcony, which overlooked the Plaza.

Kyoto was a tall, slender Japanese man wearing a brand new Santa Fe-style western outfit. On the lapel of his jacket, there was a silver and turquoise lizard pin.

"Mr. Kyoto?" Patch said.

"Ah, you must be Mr. Geronimo," he replied. "Please have a seat. I'll order you something." He spoke with only a slight accent.

Patch sat down in the white wrought iron chair across from Kyoto. Kyoto grabbed the arm of a passing waitress. Patch saw that Kyoto was having a large cappuccino.

"I'll have what he's having," Patch said to the waitress. Then he pulled out his tobacco, cigarette papers and began rolling.

"No smoking," the waitress said, and he put his tobacco paraphernia away.

"So, Mr. Kyoto, what can I do for you?" Patch asked in a friendly way.

"I am trying to recover a certain pair of, shall we say ornaments, that have been temporarily misplaced," he explained. "I'm hoping you'll be able to assist me."

"Well, I hope I can. Just what are these ornaments?"

Kyoto lowered his voice.

"They're a pair of antique Native American carvings," he whispered. "I'm sure you're already familiar with them."

He looked around to make sure no one was listening.

"I am prepared to pay the sum of five thousand dollars, on behalf of the rightful owner, for their return."

The waitress brought Patch's drink to the table, and he sipped it between words.

"And who might that be?" Patch asked just as quietly.

"Please forgive me, sir," Kyoto replied. "But I cannot answer that question at this time."

"Suit yourself," Patch responded. "But I will have to know eventually. And I'll require a small retainer up front to cover my expenses. Say, ten per cent."

"That sounds reasonable," Kyoto said. "If you'll stop by the El Dorado Hotel later this afternoon, the cash will be waiting for you at the front desk."

Patch always liked to get cash up front. It symbolized a client's commitment to the matter at hand.

"That'll be fine," he said. "And the other thing I'll need, of course, is a picture or a description of the lost items and their last known whereabouts."

The waitress brought the check and placed it on the table near Kyoto. He studied Patch for a moment, then picked it up and looked at it briefly.

"Don't play coy with me, Mr. Geronimo," he said sharply. "I believe you have all the information you need for now and a certain client of yours knows the rest."

Kyoto put the check back on the table, opened the front of his jacket and reached in for his wallet. As he did, Patch caught a glimpse of a shoulder-holstered gun.

"Please don't disappoint me in this matter," Kyoto continued. "My employer is an impatient man."

He placed a twenty dollar bill on top of the check as Patch stood to leave.

"Oh, you won't be disappointed, Mr. Kyoto," Patch reassured him. "But I wouldn't go flashing that side-arm around here. It makes the locals jumpy. I'll be by later for the cash. We'll talk again soon."

"Good day, sir. I do trust that you'll be discreet."

Patch nodded his agreement and left Kyoto at the table. Kyoto then turned toward the Plaza and, with a nod of his head, signaled to someone on the street below.

A hippyish-looking young man in a plaid shirt and jeans acknowledged the signal. He was the same young man in charge of harassing Patch the night before at the Hill of the Martyrs. His skateboard was under his arm

In a moment, Patch walked past him without notice as he headed across the crowded Plaza. The private eye's mind was focused on this new wrinkle in the case. A new piece of the puzzle, which added even more complexities to an already confusing situation.

The skateboarder jumped on his board and followed Patch, weaving back and forth trying to blend in with the crowd on the Plaza.

When he reached the front door of his apartment, Patch found a large bag attached to the door handle. Inside the bag was a book, a newspaper article and a note. The note read "Patch, hope this is what you wanted. I'm off to check on Willy. Stay out of trouble. Love, Jessie."

Patch unlocked the door and stepped inside. As he closed the door, he saw the skateboarder passing by across the street.

Once inside, Patch tossed the bag on the couch. While meeting with Kyoto, he'd received a call, but ignored it until now. He called up the message on his phone and poured himself a drink. Rachel's voice came on.

"This is Rachel. I need to talk to you very soon. It's very important. Call me."

Patch picked up the bag and plopped down on his un-made bed. Pulling the bag's contents out, he first scanned the clipping. This was the same article on antique Indian art collectors that Jessie had been reading in the office. It told of an annual gathering of Indian art collectors who came to Santa Fe each year before Indian Art Market.

Then he thumbed through the Tribal Treasures book and studied a few of the pages. Some of the prices listed for these items were astronomical. It was just like Anglos, Patch thought, to turn humble American Indian creations, which had been made to soothe one's soul and promote the well-being of a tribe, into marketable commodities. Everything was for sale these days.

It had been a long night and a long day and Patch's eyes grew tired. He rubbed them and closed his eyelids for a moment. Immediately he drifted off to sleep. In the twilight of consciousness, Patch was back at the Santa Fe boarding school pitching pennies with Willy and a couple other Native boys. It was something they often did to pass the time.

"Hey, Willy," one of the dream boys said. "I bet if I cut you open, I'd find you were stuffed with frybread."

The boy pulled out a switchblade and taunted the chubby boy. In a flash, Patch pounced on the kid and tackled him to the ground.

"Leave Willy alone!" he shouted and began pummeling the boy with punches to the face. His rage consumed him.

Suddenly, someone grabbed Patch from behind, pulling him up off the boy. He looked up to see Willy standing over him.

"Stop," Willy said. "He's been punished enough." Patch looked back down at the boy and saw, instead, himself.

Patch jerked his eyes open and shook off the dream. A quick check of the clock let him know it was 4 pm. Quickly he dialed the El Dorado Hotel.

"Benny? This is Patch. There's supposed to be an envelope for me from one of your guests there. Have you seen it? Good. Tell me, what room is Kyoto in? Thanks."

Patch got up and walked to the window. Peeking through the blinds, he saw that the skateboarder was still there. He dialed his phone again.

"Kathleen. Sorry I had to bail. Another client paged me. Everything okay there?"

"Sure, everything's fine," she said. "What about you?"

"I'm being followed," Patch said. "Anybody show up at your place?"

"No. Is there any danger?"

"Not yet. Look, we need to meet. Come to the lobby of the El Dorado Hotel. See you in ten minutes."

"What about the guy following you?"

"Did I say it was a guy?

"I just assumed," Kathleen said.

"Sure, but don't worry about me," Patch reassured her. "I can shake him."

Patch got dressed and slipped out of his placita through a side door that opened into his garage. Inside was parked an early model Indian motorcycle with a helmet slung over the handle bars. He pushed a button by the door and the garage door began to open. Walking to the bike, Patch mounted it and cranked the engine.

He eased the bike out of the garage, and the door closed behind him. A couple of revs of the engine got the bike up to speed quick. As he sped out of the driveway, Patch purposefully swerve near the skateboarder. Surprised by this maneuver, the young man fell off his skateboard.

Laying on the ground, the skateboarder fumbled around in his backpack until he came up with a gun and a cellphone. He jumped up, put the gun back in his pack and mounted the skateboard.

In his rearview mirror, Patch watched the skateboarder hurriedly place a call.

At the El Dorado, Patch retrieved the envelope from the desk clerk. It was addressed to John G. He checked inside just to make sure that the money from Kyoto was all there. Then he tucked it into his front jacket pocket.

Just then Kathleen entered the hotel wearing dark glasses, a black scarf and a black trenchcoat. She looked worried, agitated. Patch moved in beside her, took her arm and escorted her toward the elevators.

"Where are we going?" she asked, glancing around the lobby nervously.

"To meet a former business associate of yours, I suspect." The blonde became alarmed and pulled back. Patch's grip on her arm remained firm. They stepped into the elevator and the doors closed.

Neither of them spoke as they rode up to the third floor. Patch knocked on the door to room 314. Kyoto opened it. Kathleen was horrified. Kyoto was amused.

"Kathleen, this is a surprise," Kyoto said. "Won't you two come in?"

Patch pushed Kathleen toward the room. She resisted. "What have you done?" she asked Patch. There was a touch of fear in her voice.

"Bought myself some insurance, I hope."

Patch guided her into the room. Kyoto shut the door behind them. On a table near the window was a large bamboo cage. Inside, all scaly and green, was an iguana testing the air with his tongue. Kyoto sat down near the cage and tenderly stroked the lizard through the bars.

Patch sat his client down in a chair on the opposite side of the table from Kyoto. She shrank away from the lizard. Patch stood with his arms folded facing them.

"Now you two had better talk fast," Patch warned them. "The police'll be here any minute, and I'm curious about what story we'll all have to tell them."

Now both the Oriental and the Anglo became alarmed. Kyoto reached inside his coat for his gun. Patch was faster. Reaching inside his own jacket, he withdrew a well-polished Bowie knife and brandished it toward Kyoto. Kyoto froze. Patch placed the knife blade against Kyoto's neck.

"You know I just hate guns," Patch declared. "But knives are a different matter."

The Apache reached into Kyoto's coat and withdrew the gun, stuffing it in his own pocket.

"I thought we had a gentleman's agreement, Mr. Geronimo," Kyoto said.

"Oh, we do, we do," Patch replied. "You agree to talk. I agree to listen. If I like what I hear, I agree not to turn both of you over to the police for shooting my partner and murdering Jonathan Morgan."

"He can't be trusted," Kathleen said, motioning towards Kyoto. "I know him too well."

"Oh, and I suppose you've told me the whole truth, and nothing but the truth, so help you God?" Patch replied harshly.

He turned to Kyoto.

"Now let's start with these carvings you're both so interested in. How much are they worth and who do they really belong to?"

"It's hard to pin down their value, really," Kyoto replied. "Last time they changed hands for a hundred thousand dollars. Who knows what they'll bring next time."

Patch was impressed.

"Half a million bucks, huh? What makes 'em so special?"

"Scarcity, mostly," Kyoto explained. "It's the law of supply and demand. These are Zuni War Gods, and there used to be dozens on the market. Now there's just this pair, known as the Twins."

"There's more to it than that," Kathleen chimed in. "The Twins have some kind of power. They almost seem to make things happen. Make people do things. It's sort of spooky."

Patch looked at Kyoto as if to say "Is this dame loony, or what?"

"I'm afraid she's right," Kyoto said. "The Twins have a reputation for leaving a path of destruction in their wake. But they're also very seductive. Once you come near them, you want them. You're a Native American, named after a famous Apache ancestor, no doubt. I'd expect you to already know these things."

"Don't presume you know anything about Indians or me, Kyoto. Every tribe's different. Every tribal member is different. It's impossible to know everything about all of them."

Patch walked to the window and looked out.

"I grew up hearing plenty of old Apache stories of magic and superstition," Patch continued. "But that's all they were to me. Old stories. They mostly died out with my grandparents' generation."

He turned back to face Kyoto.

"Me, I'm a pragmatist."

Just then, there was a knock at the door.

"Showtime," Patch said.

He went to the door and opened it. Roybal and Johnson were standing outside.

"What's this all about, Geronimo?" Johnson asked gruffly.

"Come in, gentlemen, come in," Patch said amiably. "There are some folks here I want you to meet."

The two detectives entered the room, voicing displeasure at being taken away from their busy police duties. They eyed the lizard. The lizard eyed them back.

"May I present Sgt. Sam Roybal and Lt. Frank Johnson of the Santa Fe police department. They're working on the Morgan case I told you about."

Patch moved over beside Kathleen.

"This is my new associate, Kathleen Sykes," he said. "She's filling in until Willy gets back on his feet. Her specialty is antique American Indian art."

She nodded at the detectives, trying to conceal her surprise at Patch's unexpected explanation.

"And this is Mr. Kyoto, from San Francisco," Patch continued. "He's lost a couple of antique items of great sentimental value and has asked us to help him find them.

Kyoto gave Patch a sideways glance, then also nodded to the detectives.

"How do you do?" he said.

"Sorry, I don't know the lizard's name," Patch added, sarcastically.

"What's the bottom line here, Geronimo?" Johnson asked. "On the phone you said you had some information for us on the Morgan case."

"Oh, right. I almost forgot. I just got a tip about a guy who'll be in town for Indian Market next weekend. Seems he may know something about Willy's shooter. My guess is he'll be able to answer some questions about Morgan, too. I'll know more by the end of the week."

Johnson angled in close to Patch for effect.

"I don't know what your game is, Geronimo, but you're still high on my list," he warned. "I should haul all three of you down to the station for questioning right now. Save me a lot of time later, I'm sure."

Just then Roybal's cellphone sounded. He checked it for a text message.

"Lieutenant, we've got to go," he said. "We're late for that meeting with the Mayor you wanted."

"Relax, Johnson," Patch said. "You can talk to any of us at anytime. We'll be around."

He escorted the detectives out the door, leaving it open.

He turned back to Kathleen.

"Ms. Sykes, I believe we have some unfinished business to tend to. If you'll excuse us Mr. Kyoto, we'll leave you now. Thanks for the information."

Patch and Kathleen headed for the door.

"What about my gun?" Kyoto asked.

"Oh, that," Patch replied. "I'll leave it with the house detective on our way out. He's a friend of mine. You can pick it up from him later."

Patch and Kathleen left, closing the door behind them. Kyoto took the iguana out of the cage and caressed it lovingly.

"It's all right, pretty one," Kyoto whispered. Did the mean old policeman scare you?"

His own feelings of anxiety and frustration were soothed as he stroked the lizard's scaly skin.

5 Chapter Five

Patch woke up the next morning a little disoriented. He'd dreamt that he'd gone to bed with a lizard. He looked next to him and saw Kathleen lying asleep next to him. Parts of her nude body peaked out from the edges of the sheet.

Patch quietly covered her and got up. She stirred a little, but didn't wake. Their clothes were strewn around the bed and on the floor. He went to the closet, found a pair of sweat pants and put them on. What he needed was coffee.

While the coffee brewed, he took a quick shower. The water, as always, washed the sins of the night away. Stepping out of the shower, he wrapped a towel around himself. The smell of fresh-brewed caffeine reached his nostrils and began to awaken a few more brain cells.Using a second towel to dry his hair, he walked back to the kitchenette where he found Kathleen, wearing nothing but his shirt, pouring two cups of coffee.

"Patch," she said, handing him a cup. "How'd you get that nickname?"

She sat down on the couch. Patch followed.

"When I was a kid—before I went to boarding school—we lived in a little redneck town in southern New Mexico. The Anglo kids called me Apache and ran around hoopin' and hollerin' like Indians in the movies used to do."

He mimicked the Hollywood Indian war whoop.

"Anyway, Apache got shortened to just Patch and it stuck with me. It kind of became a badge of honor, even though they meant it as a put down."

She smiled.

"I see how you can turn situations to your favor. You're so unpredictable. You had me worried there for a minute at Kyoto's hotel."

"Speaking of which, how'd you get mixed up with that lizard man and this whole business?"

Kathleen shifted a little and looked away.

"I don't know. I studied primitive art in college and when I got out, the only jobs I could get were with museums and Indian art collectors."

She looked back at Patch.

"It's been okay, I guess. You get to travel, rub elbows with the rich and famous who like to spend their money collecting indigenous artifacts."

"You mean the cultural and religious property of American Indian people," Patch corrected her. "But go on."

"When I went to work for Ryan Coulter," she continued, "I didn't know he had a sideline business dealing in black market items. Kyoto is one of his "buyers," as he calls them."

Patch put his coffee cup down on a nearby end table and got up.

"Fancy word for grave robber, if you ask me," he said as he walked to the kitchenette.

"I thought you didn't believe in Indian superstitions."

Patch opened the cabinet door and took out the bottle and poured a little of the clear liquid into his coffee.

"I don't," he answered angrily. "But I do believe in peoples' right to be left alone, their right to live out their lives with whatever dignity has been left them after generations of colonization and genocide."

He downed the coffee and poured himself another.

Kathleen was taken aback by Patch's sudden shift in mood. She clutched the shirt around her and leaned back against the arm of the couch. Patch's phone rang. He recovered his own composure and answered.

"Hello. Oh, hi, Jessie. What's up?"

"You'd better drop who or what you're doing and get over here," she said with a nervous edge. "Somebody broke in the office. The place is a mess. And the Indian elder is back. Says he won't leave until he sees you."

"All right, Jessie, take it easy. Offer the man a cup of coffee. I'll be right there."

Jessie hung up and smiled at the old man who was seated across the front office on the couch. He was dressed in a traditional Pueblo man's shirt with a turquoise bandana around his head. A finger-woven belt with tassels encircled his waist. Large pieces of turquoise jewelry adorned his hands. He smiled back.

"Mr. Geronimo is on his way," she said.

"Good," the elder replied with a smile.

"Want some coffee?" she asked.

He nodded. So Jessie made her way through the overturned furniture and random chaos of papers to the area where the coffee maker used to be. Mumbling to herself, she located the coffee maker in the rubble and placed it back on it's stand.

"I'll be right back," she said, excusing herself to get some water.

Meanwhile, across town at the hospital, Willy stirred in his bed. Suddenly his eyes flew open and began searching the room. His life-support monitors immediately sent a signal to the nurses station. At the same time, Willy found the call button and pressed it incessantly. The duty nurse rushed to his room.

"I'm as hungry as an elk in mating season," Willy blurted out to her. "Got any food?"

The nurse picked up the room phone and dialed it.

"Doctor," she said. "Your patient is awake."

A few minutes later, Patch arrived at his office. The Native elder was patiently sipping his coffee. Patch quickly surveyed the damage, then walked over to the man and extended his hand.

"I'm John Geronimo. Sorry to keep you waiting."

The old man shook his hand once, softly, in the Indian way, without speaking.

"Come inside my office where we can talk." Patch led the way, opening his inner office door. Peering inside, he found more wreckage.

"Please excuse the mess," Patch said to the elder. "I think an interior design critic was here."

The old man didn't laugh. Neither did Patch.

He stepped in, found an overturned chair and set it upright. He indicated to the old man that he should sit there. Then Patch stepped behind his desk and set his own chair back in its place. Jessie stood in the doorway.

"Jessie, call my attorney and tell him what's happened here."

She nodded and started to move.

"Oh, and call the insurance agent to see if we're covered for this type of... thing."

She nodded again and backed out, closing the door. Patch then turned his attention to the old man who had been waiting for his turn to speak.

"Now what can I do for you, Mr. uh..."

"My name is not important," the elder said. "But it is Abraham Seumptewa. I am a Bow Priest from the Pueblo of Zuni. I have come to you with a religious matter of great importance and urgency to my people. We need your help."

"I don't have a lot of experience with religious matters, Mr. Seumptewa," Patch replied. "I don't see how I could help."

"You can call me Abe."

"Okay, Abe. What makes you think I'm the right man for the job?"

"Each spring the priests of our clan carve the likenesses of two guardian spirits which are placed at sacred locations in the hills of our reservation," Abe said. "This we have been doing since the time of our emergence as a people. In our language, these guardian spirits are called Big Brother and Little Brother. In the outside world, they're known as the twin War Gods. Maybe you've heard of them."

"Heard of them?" Patch said with a sarcastic chuckle. "For the last three days, that's all I've heard about. They seem to have taken over my life and turned everything upside down."

"Then I have come to the right man," Abe said. "During the last few decades, many of these War Gods have been stolen from our people in various ways. They've become valuable art objects to outsiders. But to us they are living beings who protect our tribe and maintain balance in the world. Their home is with us."

As the elder spoke, Patch began rolling himself a cigarette.

"Today," Abe continued, "the last of our missing Brothers is leaving New York City to begin their journey home. A generous benefactor secured the Twins from a European collector and donated them back to our tribe. A company called Interstate Security Transport has been hired by the tribe bring them to us. My brother, Luther, is also a Bow Priest, and he is traveling with them as they make their way here to Santa Fe."

"They're coming here?" Patch asked. "What for? Why don't you just have them delivered straight to Zuni?"

"They've been, how should I say–polluted–by the outside world and must be purified before they can be returned home. My brother and I are to perform the ceremony at a gallery here in Santa Fe owned by one of our tribal members."

Patch lit the freshly rolled cigarette and took a puff. "It sounds like you have things pretty much under control. What do you need me for?"

"Two attempts have been made to steal the Brothers since they arrived in New York. Both attempts failed, but there are those who will stop at nothing to get their hands on the Guardians. We can't afford to take any more chances. Our tribe's welfare is at stake. The world's balance is in jeopardy."

Patch was about to object again when Jessie opened the office door. Patch looked up.

"The hospital's calling," she said. "Willy's awake and he's asking for you."

Patch immediately stood up.

"That's great news," he said. "Tell 'em I'll be right there." Turning back to Abe, Patch said, "Mr. Seumptewa–Abe. I'll have to think about this. It's a little bit outside my turf. It sounds like you need help from the FBI or somebody."

Patch stood up and shook Abe's hand. The old man wouldn't let go.

"We want to handle this from inside the Native community, and we don't have much time," he said, seriously.

"How much did you say this job pays?"

"We have no money, Mr. Geronimo."

Patch broke off the handshake and headed for the door.

"You really drive a hard bargain," he said.

"I know you'll take this case," the elder said with a smile.

Patch paused at the door.

"Oh, how's that?"

"The spirits are never wrong."

Patch frowned.

"We'll see. Leave a phone number where I can reach you. I'll let you know this afternoon."

He left the office, but Abe's knowing smile haunted Patch all the way to the hospital.

At the hospital, he found Rachel pacing in the hallway outside Willy's room. Mrs. Chino, Willy and Rachel's mother, was sitting in a chair next to the door to his room. Rachel saw Patch coming down the hall and ran to him.

"Oh, Patch, Willy's going to be all right," she announced.

"That's what I heard. Can I see him now?"

"Yeah, he wants to talk to you, but he's been rambling on about some vision he had while he was unconscious," Rachel said. "See for yourself."

Patch greeted Mrs. Chino respectfully and then he and Rachel entered the room. Willy was sitting up in bed. His chest was all bandaged up, and there were tubes in his arms. He was wild-eyed and beaming, eating green jello.

"Patch, it was awesome," Willy said enthusiastically. "I think I had one of those near-death things that people talk about."

"That's good, Willy," Patch said. "I want to hear all about it when you're better. The important thing now is that you do what the doctor tells you. I bet that includes not getting too excited."

Willy wouldn't be deterred.

"No, you don't understand. I went down this tunnel, see. And I came out on top of Black Mesa, you know, over at the Pueblo. And there were these two bright twin lights. And they were talking to me. I don't remember exactly what they said, but I do know there's an old Indian guy who wants you to do something real important, and you gotta do it. They said you gotta do it. It was your destiny, they said."

Willy's whole being was filled with energy. He almost glowed. Patch hadn't seen his friend this excited since the time they ran away from boarding school together.

Patch's mind began racing. How could Willy have known about Mr. Seumptewa? And the twin lights. They spoke to Willy? Impossible. Patch had to get some fresh air and sort this all out.

"Now you get some rest," he admonished. "And stay off the sugar. It's making you hallucinate."

He patted Willy on the arm and left the room. Rachel followed.

Willy called to him.

"Hey, Patch, don't leave."

He looked at the nurse.

"Can I have some more jello?"

Out in the hall, Patch leaned against the wall for support. He was having trouble breathing.

"What's wrong?" Rachel asked.

"I feel like I'm in the eye of a hurricane. Everything about this case is swirling around me. It doesn't make any sense. Or maybe it makes too much sense."

He looked at Rachel and lowered his voice.

"You know how devoutly non-religious I am."

He took a deep breath and calmed himself down.

"Just tell Willy I got the message, but I had to go."

He marched off down the hall leaving Rachel wondering about Patch's state of mind.

The private eye went straight to the El Dorado Hotel. He entered the lobby and headed for the phones just past a large bench. He noticed the skateboarder sitting on the bench reading a copy of Rolling Stone magazine.

Patch picked up the house phone.

"Mr. Kyoto, please. Room 314."

As he waited, he casually shifted around to face the bench. The skateboarder appeared to be engrossed in his magazine. A few moments passed and the operator came on the line.

"I'm sorry, but there's no answer."

Patch thanked her and put down the phone. He decided it was time to confront his shadow.

He sat down on the bench next to the skateboarder. The young man did not look up. Patch stared openly at him and took out his rolling papers and tobacco.

"Where is he?" Patch asked, pouring tobacco into a slightly curved rolling paper. The youth lowered his magazine and looked vaguely in Patch's direction.

"You talkin' to me?" the young man asked.

Still busy with his cigarette, Patch said, "Yes, I am. Where is he?"

"Where is who?"

"You know who. Kyoto."

The youth lifted his gaze up to meet Patch's eyes.

"Never heard of him."

Patch licked his neatly rolled cigarette and smiled amiably.

"Do you work for Kyoto or Coulter, or both?"

The youth went back to his magazine.

"Shove off."

Patch lit his cigarette and leaned back comfortably on the bench.

"You'll have to talk to me sooner or later, and you can tell your boss I said so."

Patch spotted his friend, Jake, the El Dorado house detective. He had been standing against a near-by corner post watching them the whole time.

At that moment, for some odd reason, Patch realized that he and all of his colleagues were lurkers, paid to lay low and hover. They were part of society's collective shadow, existing to help make proper folk continue to appear proper. A curious revelation, Patch thought, coming at a curious time. But he moved on.

Patch signaled Jake to come over. He rose from the bench and shook Jake's hand.

"Hello, Patch," Jake said. "How's Willy doing?"

"He's gonna make it, Jake. Thanks for asking."

Patch nodded toward the skateboarder.

"Say, how come you let riff-raff like this hang around such a swank hotel?"

"Not much I can do unless he's causing trouble," Jake replied.

"I bet if you take a look in that backpack of his, you'll find a piece."

"Oh, really."

Jake took a step toward the kid.

"Let me see your pack, son."

"Keep your hands to yourself," the young man said as he stood up.

"If you don't cooperate, I'll have to ask you to leave."

"I won't forget you guys," the skateboarder said and stomped off toward the front exit.

When he was safely out of range, Jake said, "What was that about?"

"He's been tailing me. I think he's somehow tied to Willy's shooter."

Patch started after him. Turning back to Jake he said, "Keep your eyes peeled for me?"

"Sure thing," Jake said with a nod.

As the youth reached the front doors, Kyoto, looking tired and haggard, entered the hotel. Kyoto noticed the skateboarder, but the youth nodded his head towards Patch and kept walking. Kyoto approached Patch.

"There you are," Patch said. "You don't look so good."

"I've been down at police headquarters," Kyoto said, wiping his forehead with his handkerchief.

"What were you doing down there?"

"Answering questions. They just released me a few minutes ago."

"What did you tell 'em?"

"Not a thing. They seemed most interested in finding out what you were up to. I followed the story line you had indicated earlier in my room."

"Good, good. I was going to ask a few questions of my own, but you appear to be all questioned out. I'll keep you posted if there's any news."

Patch turned abruptly and left. Something told him it was time to check in at the office.

Jessie had just about finished straightening up the mess in the office. She was on the phone when Patch got there. Her lips formed a silent "Rachel" as she pointed to the phone. Patch shook his head indicating that he didn't want to talk to her right now.

"No, not yet," she spoke into the receiver. "Have you tried his cell?"

Patch nodded to Jessie to indicate that he had missed calls from Rachel on his phone.

"Yes, I'll have him call as soon as he comes in," the secretary told Willy's sister before hanging up.

Patch poured himself a cup of coffee.

"I can't keep your girlfriends from finding out about each other much longer," Jessie said. "Ms. Barkley's in there," she continued, motioning toward the inner office with her lips.

Patch took a sip of the coffee.

"What else?"

"I called Mr. Seumptewa like you asked me to. He said to meet him at the Butterfly Gallery at 5 pm."

Patch nodded.

"And a Mr. Coulter called, long distance. When I told him you weren't in, he said to tell you that the young man gave him the message, and that he'll phone again."

Patch grinned.

"Coulter, huh. Things are getting very interesting, Jessie. Oh, thanks for straightening up around here. I don't know what I'd do without you."

"You'd crash and burn is what you'd do," she said with a smile.

Patch opened the door to his inner office and went in. It, too, had been partially put back in order.

Kathleen Sykes, dressed as on her first visit to the office, rose from the chair beside his desk and came quickly toward him. She was panicked.

"Somebody's been in my apartment!" she said. "It's turned upside down. You must've let somebody follow you there."

"No, I shook him before I got to your place. The same interior decorator stopped by here." More to himself than to her, he said, "I wonder if it could be Kyoto. He was away from his hotel for quite awhile. He told me he'd been answering police questions."

"You went to see Kyoto?" Kathleen asked with alarm. "What for?"

He put an arm around her shoulders and led her over to his swivel chair.

"Because, sweets, I've got to keep in touch with all the loose ends of this dizzying mess if I'm ever going to get to the bottom of it."

He lightly kissed her on the forehead and sat her down.

"Now, we've got to find a new home for you, haven't we?"

"I certainly can't go back to my place."

Patch thought for a moment.

"I think I've got it. Wait a minute."

He went into the outer office and shut the door behind him.

"Jessie, what does your woman's intuition tell you about her?" He cocked his head towards his inner office.

"That she's manipulative, deceptive and untrustworthy," she immediately responded.

"That's clear enough. Are you sure it's your intuition talking, and not something else?"

Jessie blushed a little.

"Why do you ask?"

"Because I need a place to stash her for awhile."

"You mean my house?"

Patch nodded.

"She's in danger?"

"Probably."

Jessie fiddled with her fingernail for a minute while she thought about it.

"Well, somebody needs to keep an eye on her, for your sake."

"Keep your friends close, and your enemies even closer, the old saying goes."

"I'd have to tell my mom something other than this woman might be in danger," she finally said. "That would scare her. Maybe I could say she's a surprise witness or something that you need to keep under wraps until the last minute."

"That's my girl," Patch said with a smile.

He opened the door to the inner office and smiled across the threshold to Kathleen.

"Jessie is going to put you up at her place for a few days."

Kathleen, coming out of the door, turned grateful eyes on Jessie.

"That's very kind of you," she said.

"No problem, Ms. Barkley," Jessie said trying to conceal her true feelings about the whole thing.

"Oh, I forgot," Patch said. "You two haven't been properly introduced. Jessie Medina, this is Kathleen Sykes. Kathleen's in the antique art business. The cops think she's temporarily working for us. Now, you two had better get going."

Jessie started collecting her things.

"Go out the back way to Water Street," Patch instructed. "Take a cab to the main cab office. Switch cabs and then go to your place. Keep your eyes open for a tail."

He turned to Kathleen.

"I'll call you later," he said in a more intimate voice.

Jessie mined a world of information from that one interaction. She gave her boss a disapproving look before heading out the office door.

Patch stepped back into his inner office and looked around the room. He straightened a picture that hung crookedly on the wall. The phone rang.

"Eagle Eye... Yes, this is Geronimo."

It was Ryan Coulter.

"I've been waiting to hear from you, Mr. Coulter. Yes, I'd like to meet—the sooner, the better. So you're in town already. In fifteen minutes? Sure. La Posoda Hotel, Room thirteen."

Patch jumped on his Indian bike and headed for the hotel. La Posada was a collection of individual adobe suites scattered over an couple of acres, interspersed with lush vegetation. It was a quaint, quasi-historic location the tourists just loved.

Like so many other Santa Fe destinations, it offered members of a stressful corporate culture a band-aid for the soul. To Patch's jaded sensibilities, it was just one more example of Santa Fe's successful and long-running tourism marketing campaign.

He parked his bike in one of the small parking areas inside the complex and walked to cottage number thirteen. He knocked on the door. It was opened by the now familiar skateboarder, who stepped aside and said nothing. Patch entered the room.

A large, overweight man struggled to raise himself up out of a plush armchair. He finally succeeded. Even though he was wearing loose-fitting summer clothes, he was sweating. He crossed the room to meet Patch.

"Ah, Mr. Geronimo. Finally we meet," Coulter said. "I've heard so much about you."

He extended his hand. It was cold and clammy. Patch politely shook it once.

"Mr. Coulter," was all Patch said.

"Would you mind terribly if I just called you Mr. G for short?" Coulter asked.

"Call me whatever you like," Patch replied.

Holding on to Patch's hand, Coulter put his other hand on Patch's elbow and guided him to a chair close to the plush armchair. Next to the chair was a table. On that table was a silver tray that held a bottle of Scotch, two glasses and a box of cigars.

Coulter began pouring Scotch into a glass that was meant for Patch. The chubby man watched his guest as he poured. Patch watched without response.

The skateboarder went into an adjacent room and closed the door. Coulter offered the half full glass to Patch.

"I like a man who doesn't say when," Coulter commented. "Its the sign of someone who's sure of himself and unconcerned with social appearances."

Patch took the glass, offering a courteous smile in return. Coulter raised his glass and examined the drink's clarity.

"Well, here's to straight talk and transparent meanings," he said. They both drank.

"You're a man of few words," Coulter said wiping his lips.

"On the contrary," Patch replied. "I like to talk, when talk's called for. But I don't find silence awkward either."

"Splendid," Coulter said loudly. "I also like a man who knows when to speak his mind and when to hold his tongue."

Coulter picked up the box of cigars and held it out to Patch. Patch took one, sniffed it and trimmed the end off, using a cutter also on the silver tray. Picking up a gold lighter from the tray, he lit the cigar and took a long slow drag. It was smooth and aromatic.

Coulter pulled his chair closer to Patch, took a cigar from the box and lowered himself into the chair. He smiled comfortably.

"Now, sir, let's talk," he said.

"What shall we talk about?" Patch said coyly. "The Twins, perhaps?"

Coulter's fat jiggled with laughter. His face radiated with delight.

"Everything up front and out in the open. Is that it? Yes, by all means, let's talk about the Twins."

Then his tone became serious.

"But first, answer me one question. Are you here as Ms. Sykes' representative?"

Patch gazed thoughtfully at the ash-tipped end of his cigar.

"That's still up in the air," he replied. "It depends."

"On what?" Coulter prodded.

Patch blew a plume of smoke up in the air.

"Several things," Patch returned evasively.

"Does Mr. Kyoto have anything to do with it?"

"Maybe. Maybe not."

"Come, come. Mr. G. Who else is there to consider?"

"There's me. Myself."

Coulter sank back in his chair, blowing out his breath in a long robust sigh of relief.

"Perfect," he said. "I do like a man who tells you right out that he's looking after himself. Don't we all look out for ourselves? I don't trust a man who says otherwise."

"Uh-huh," Patch said, confidently puffing on his cigar. "Now let's talk about the Twins."

"Let's, G," Coulter said. "Do you have any concept of how much money can be gotten for them?"

"Not really. I've only heard guesses."

"Well, if told you half the price, you'd call me a liar."

"Try me."

"How much did Kyoto offer you for it's return?" Coulter quizzed.

"Ten thousand," Patch lied.

"Ten thousand? Only ten thousand?" Thinking out loud, Coulter said, "They must know what they are, how much they're really worth. But do they?"

He cleared his throat.

"What is your impression? Do Sykes and Kyoto know what the twins are worth or what they represent?"

"They seemed to. Kyoto said they brought a hundred thousand bucks, and they had some spooky powers."

Coulter laughed uproariously.

"Well, I dare say that they either don't really know what's at stake here or they chose not to tell you."

He thought out loud again.

"If they don't know, then I may be the only one in the entire world still alive who does know."

"That's great," Patch said. "When you tell me, that'll make two of us."

Coulter squinted his eyes at Patch.

"That's mathematically correct, but I'm not sure I'm going to tell you."

"Don't be foolish, Mr. Coulter. You know what they're worth and why. I know where they can be found. That's why I'm here."

"Well, where are they?" Coulter demanded.

"It's too early to tell. You know they're not in my office." Coulter smiled.

"You see how you are? You want me to tell you what I know, but you won't tell me what you know. That's hardly a fair exchange. I'm afraid we won't be able to do business along these lines."

Patch dropped all the pleasantries. He gave Coulter a hard look as he stood up.

"Think again, Mr. Coulter. Think good and hard. Today's the day to do business, or we won't be doing business at all. I can get along just fine without you."

Patch angrily threw his glass into the corner Kiva fireplace. It shattered, but neither he nor Coulter took notice.

"And another thing—"

Patch was interrupted by the sound of the bedroom door opening. The skateboarder came into the room, shutting the door behind him. He stood like a guard monitoring the situation.

"And another thing," Patch continued. "Keep that gun-toting punk under control while you're making up your mind. I don't want to have to kill him."

The youth didn't move a muscle.

Coulter laughed.

"My, but that's quite a temper you have, Mr. G."

"You ain't seen the half of it, Coulter. I get really mad when I'm being toyed with."

Patch moved toward the door to leave.

"I have another meeting to go to," he said. "Think it over. I'll give you until 9 o'clock tomorrow morning. Then you're either in or out, for good."

He glared at Coulter, then left, slamming the door behind him.

As Patch reached his motorcycle, he put two fingers inside his collar and pulled it away from his throat. His mouth was dry. He licked his lips to moisten them. He took out his handkerchief and wiped his face. He looked down at his hands. They were trembling. He grinned to himself as he put on his helmet. He had done it. He had pulled off a risky con on an accomplished con artist.

Starting the engine, the private detective backed out of the parking space. As he left the hotel parking lot, Kyoto passed through the hotel's main lobby and headed toward Coulter's suite. Neither man saw the other.

When Patch got to the Butterfly Gallery, he found several people milling around with drinks in their hands looking at the American Indian artwork hanging on the walls. It was just a few days before Indian Market, the time of year when all the galleries in town put on wine and cheese parties for their patrons and displayed the latest in Native works of art.

Even though was was a partitime artist himself, Patch wasn't sure he approved of the whole notion of Indians painting pretty pictures to decorate the walls of rich white people. It wasn't that he was against Indians making good money. On the contrary, he was all for it. It was just that Europeans, then Americans, had done everything they could to wipe American Indians off the face of the earth so they could inhabit the promise land. Nowadays these immigrants wandered why so many Natives had lost touch with their cultures. Like everything else in Indian-white relations, it was complicated.

Patch wove his way through the crowd until he found the bar where he ordered a mixed drink. Taking a few sips, he wandered through the gallery until he located Abe who was talking to small circle of non-Indians in the corner of the gallery.

Abe excused himself from the group and led Patch to a secluded back room of the gallery.

"I'm glad to see you, Geronimo. Have you reached a decision concerning my request for help?"

"Yes, sir, I have. My partner came back from the dead just to tell me I had to help you, so here I am. Pretty persuasive stuff."

"The Guardians are very powerful medicine," Abe admonished. "They will reward you in their own way for your assistance. And they can bring misfortune to those who don't treat them with respect. But, gladly, they are almost ready to begin their journey home."

"That's good, because dangerous men are after your Guardians, and they seem to think that the pair are worth any price."

"I am aware of the danger. But you, Mr. Geronimo, must be aware of the curious side effects the Guardians have on people. Your motives must be pure. And we must perform a protection ceremony for you and anyone who will come in contact with them."

"No need to do a ceremony for my benefit," Patch said after downing his drink. "But I won't prevent anyone else from taking you up on the offer. What I need is a map of the travel route and the names and numbers of the security team."

"Of course. That information is out front in my truck. Let's take care of it right now." Patch sucked out the last drop of his drink, placed the glass on a nearby counter, and followed Abe out to the street.

Abe led him to an older model turquoise Chevrolet Apache pickup parked in front of the gallery. Patch was very impressed with Abe's set of wheels. He looked it over from bumper to bumper.

"It belongs to my brother, Luther," Abe said. "I'm using it until he returns with the Guardians."

Abe unlocked the driver's side and removed a rather worn, brown briefcase from the front seat. While Patch was waiting for Abe to get the papers, he noticed a dark-colored limo slowly cruising by.

Abe handed Patch the map and contact information.

"The return of the Guardians means everything to us, Geronimo. At least allow us to pray for your success on our behalf."

"Suit yourself. I'll focus on logistics and leave the praying to you," Patch said.

"I will be visiting your partner at the hospital to perform a special blessing ritual for him. The twin spirits very rarely appear to Zuni Bow Priests, much less anyone outside our pueblo. Your partner must be a pure soul. He, of course, will be our invited guest at all future Zuni feast days."

"Willy is special all right," Patch admitted. "That is one thing we can agree on."

They shook hands, and Patch started down the sidewalk.

As he walked, he noticed that the limo was following him. It stopped in the street and the back door opened. A woman's voice called out from inside.

"Geronimo!"

This stopped Patch cold in his tracks. He walked over and peered into the open door. A smile came to his face as he stepped into the limo, closing the door behind him.

He sat down across from an attractive forty-something woman he knew. She was dressed in formal evening attire. She poured Patch a glass of champagne and handed it to him.

"Ride with me, Geronimo," the woman said. "I need to talk to you. Pardon the fanfare. I'm on my way to the opera."

She motioned to the driver, and the limo pulled away.

"Life's been good to you Melissa—excuse me, Ms. District Attorney. How long has it been?"

"Ever since you dropped out of the legal business. Do you ever regret that decision?"

"About once a month when I can't pay my bills. But I know you didn't go to the trouble of finding me just to talk about old times. What can a lowly Apache P.I. like myself do for you?"

"I was hoping you could tell me who killed Mr. Morgan."

"Ha. That's a good one. Sorry. I really don't know."

"But I bet you could make an excellent guess."

"My guess might be excellent or my guess might be crummy, but my mama didn't raise any little Indians dopey enough to make guesses like that to a district attorney. You wearing a wire somewhere under that gown?"

"Now don't be like that, Geronimo," she said with a cute little fake pout. "It's just that I've got people downtown who're anxious to see some results on this case. Unsolved murders are hard on the tourism industry. I thought you could help me, informally. That's all. How's Willy?"

"He's gonna be fine, thanks. And I don't mind if you want to make it formal. I'll be happy to come down to your office and make a statement anytime. But you can just drop me off at the next corner, for now."

He downed the rest of his champagne.

Melissa motioned to the driver, then leaned towards Patch and touched his leg.

"Patch, I'm trying to keep you out of this for old times sake. But you've got to help me. If you're withholding evidence..."

Patch lifted her hand off his leg, kissed it and placed it on her knee. The limo stopped and Patch opened the door. He paused before getting out.

"In case you've forgotten, my clients are entitled to privacy," he reminded her. "And as far as I can see, my best chance of clearing myself of this trouble is by bringing in the murderer, or murderers, all neatly tied up. And my only chance of doing that to stay away from you and the police because you'll only gum up the works. See my point of view?"

He stepped out of the limo.

Just as he was about to close the limo door, he paused and said, "Look me up sometime when you're not wearing your D. A. uniform. We'll relive some old times."

He shut the door, and the limo drove away.

"Women!" Patch said under his breath, and resumed his journey on foot.

Ambling northward, he basked in the golden glow of another sunset as it projected its multi-colored light show on Santa Fe's adobe walls.

In the distance, the bells of St. Francis Cathedral chimed. Patch realized that he had a lot to do in a very short time. Shifting mental gears, he picked up his pace and headed for home.

When he arrived, he turned on the lamp next to his bed and fished his little black address book out of the top drawer of his night stand. He flipped through the pages until he came to the letter "M." His finger slid down the page, stopping at the name Mangas Coloradas Montoya, whose nickname was Red. He pulled his cellphone out and dialed. In a few moments, a voice said, "Yo."

"Red, this is Geronimo," Patch said.

"Hey, man, what's happnin'?" Montoya answered. "Long time, no see."

"You know that favor you owe me? I need to collect on it right now, bro. It's important."

Hearing the seriousness of Patch's request, his old friend replied, "Anything. You know that."

Patch explained the situation.

"I need you and Billy to be on a plane and in St. Louis before morning to bring back some heavy tribal medicine to Santa Fe."

6 Chapter Six

The morning sun reflected majestically off the stainless steel arch that symbolized St. Louis. In the heart of the city's industrial district, two empty vans were parked side by side in the Interstate Transport loading bay awaiting their cargo. One was a brand new official-looking sleek grey vehicle with the words "Interstate Transport" painted on the sides. The other was a dented white junkyard reject that appeared to have just come from a round of demolition derby.

Two identical crates rested on the loading dock behind the vans. Both were marked "Property of the Zuni Tribe."

One crate contained a black bag, tied with a draw string, about three feet long and two feet wide. Inside that bag were the objects around which this whole drama pivoted: the Twin War Gods. Because of their size, shape and weight, they bore remarkable resemblance to Torah Scrolls used by Jewish congregations all over the world. To the Zunis, these objects were just as sacred, and, like the legendary lost tribes of Israel, yearned to rejoin their Zuni brothers in their ancient homeland.

The other crate contained an identical black bag tied with an identical draw string. In every external detail, this package was identical to the one in the neighboring crate. Only this bag contained two very secular logs. Decoys.

As the two crates were about to be closed up, an elderly American Indian man stepped from the shadows. He himself was almost the twin of Abe Seumptewa who was back in Santa Fe. Appearing beside this Zuni Elder were two younger long-haired Apache men with rifles: Red and Billy. They checked over everything, making sure it was safe for the old man to proceed.

"Just a minute," the elder said to the dock workers. He removed a small leather pouch from the medicine bag that was strapped over his shoulder. Reaching inside the little pouch, he removed just a pinch of its powdery yellow contents. He repeated a short Zuni prayer as he sprinkled the powder over the crate bearing the real Twins. When he finished, he closed up the bag of corn meal and put it back in his pocket.

"You're next," he said to the two Apaches.

They came closer to the old man as he withdrew a feather fan, a bundle of sage and a lighter from the medicine bag. He put the lighter's flame to the tip of the sage, and thick white smoke began to rise from it. Using the feather, he wafted the smoke over the two Apaches. This process appeared very similar to Victoria Stanford's earlier smudging ceremony, but this was the real deal.

Once the Zuni Bow Priest was satisfied with the cleasing, the then brought out a sprig of cedar from the bag and lit it. This smoke, too, was guided over the two Apaches in the final bit of ritual to prepare them for the journey ahead.

"Now we're ready," Luther said to the dock workers who then quickly finished packing protective styrofoam forms around the bags in the twin crates. Then, using nail guns, they sealed the lids on both crates.

The fake crate, the one holding the logs, was then loaded into the grey, official-looking Interstate Transport van.

"It's time to get going, Luther," Red said. "I'll help you into the van."

They walked to the passenger's side of the fancy decoy van. The younger helped the elder into his seat.

"I can tell that the Twins are radiating their powerful energies now," Luther said with a chuckle. "It's not every day that an Apache warrior named Mangas Coloradoas helps an old Zuni get his guardian gods back home."

"I guess it proves just how powerful the Guardians really are," Red replied. "You take care now."

He shut the door as a Security Transport driver slipped in behind the steering wheel and a uniformed armed guard climbed in back.

Red took up his position in the back of the other van, where the other crate had already been loaded. The other Apache, Billy, started up the engine. With a nod from Red, both vans pulled out of the loading bay and into the street, each going its separate way.

Back in Santa Fe the honking of a loud and insistent car horn woke Patch from a deep and much needed sleep. He sat up in bed, checking to see if there was anyone next to him. Sometimes he just couldn't remember in the morning what he'd done the night before.

The horn sounded again. Patch stumbled to the window and peaked out through the blinds. A white Cadillac convertible with the top down sat at the curb. The skateboarder, Patch's favorite person in the whole world, was in the driver's seat.

"Shit," Patch said through clenched teeth. The kid, a real slacker if Patch had ever seen one, hopped out of the car. Patch opened his front door as the kid approached.

"Come on. He wants to see you," the punk said.

"Traded in your skateboard, I see." Patch replied dryly. "Hope you got a good deal."

"Cut the wise-cracks and get dressed."

"I see you haven't lost your charm, either. Wait here. I'll be right out."

Patch closed the door and went to get dressed, leaving the slacker outside to cool his heels. Returning to the car, the skateboarder scanned his radio station options and finally settled on a hip-hop rendition of Bob Dylan's "The Times They Are A Changing." He cranked it up loud enough for Patch to hear inside.

Wanting to spare his neighbors any prolonged unpleasantness, Patch dress quickly and exited the apartment. He hopped in the back seat of the Cadi convertible without opening the door, and the car sped away.

At the La Posada Hotel, the young man parked the car and got out. Patch jumped out of the back seat and followed. As they neared Coulter's hotel door, Patch purposefully lagged behind the young man a little. Suddenly, the Apache grabbed the youth from behind and pinned his arms back. He reached inside the youth's jacket and withdrew two pistols.

"Didn't your mama tell you never to play with guns?" Patch asked sarcastically.

The skateboarder quit struggling, and Patch pushed him toward the door while putting the guns inside his own jacket. The youth opened the door and stepped into the suite. Patch followed.

Coulter entered from the bedroom, closing the door behind him. Patch caught a quick glimpse of a man in a suit sitting at a table in the bedroom. Coulter approached Patch. The youth stared at the floor.

"Come in, come in, and thank you for coming," Coulter said. Patch pulled the guns from his jacket and handed them to Coulter.

"Here. You shouldn't let him play with these. He could hurt himself."

Taking the pistols, Coulter laughed uproariously.

"Well, well, you are an unpredictable man, Mr. G."

Coulter handed the pistols to the youth and motioned for him to go into the other room. Coulter led Patch to the bar and mixed him a drink.

"I apologize for the young man's behavior. Good help is so hard to find."

"Forget it," Patch retorted. "Let's get down to business."

"All right then," Coulter said. He offered Patch a drink.

"It's a little early for me, but you go ahead," Patch said.

"I was hoping we could celebrate our new partnership," Coulter said as he filled two glasses. "You can produce the Twins, can't you?"

"In a day or two," Patch replied.

"All right then, a day or two it shall be," Coulter said agreeably. He put a drink in Patch's hand and gestured toward the chairs. They sat. Holding up his glass, he said, "Here's to a fair bargain and large profits for both of us." He took a drink. Patch didn't.

"And what's your idea of a fair bargain?" Patch inquired.

"Twenty-five thousand upon delivery of the Twins to me, and another twenty five thousand later, after we've 'liquidated' our holdings."

"Sounds good."

Patch downed his drink.

"So what makes this pair of War Gods so pricy?"

He passed his glass to Coulter, who dutifully refilled it.

"Just the best kept secret in the Indian antiquities business," Coulter remarked. "The Twins have added value."

He handed the glass back to Patch. He sipped at it.

"Added value," the P.I. said. "What added value?"

Coulter picked up a manila envelope from a nearby table and removed an eight by ten photo. He handed the photo to Patch, who looked at it briefly. He saw a pair of slightly weathered wooden Zuni War Gods with only the barest hints of arms or legs or other features.

"Zuni War Gods are remarkably plain and unadorned," Coulter explained. "Nothing like the ornately carved Kachinas made by the Hopi. War Gods work their magic, so to speak, as they weather and disintegrate in the sun, wind and rain."

Patch put the photo back on the table.

"So I've heard."

"These particular War Gods are the oldest in circulation," Coulter continued. "Now, of course, they're the only ones still on the market."

Patch began to feel a little funny. His speech began to slur a little.

"So, I'm still waiting for the bottom line here," he said. "None of this is really news, and none of it would account for the outrageous asking price."

"Very astute, Mr. G," Coulter replied. "The Twins have a reputation for causing trouble, mischief really, for their owners."

"Come on Coulter. Tell me something I don't know."

"Bear with me. I'm getting there. So, partly as a peace offering to the spirit of the Twins, and partly because of their plainness, various owners down through the years have added their own valuable touches to the statues."

"Touches? What kind of touches?"

"Emeralds, diamonds and rubies. Valuable additions."

Patch rubbed his eyes and shook his head.

"What?" said Patch. "I'm not getting this."

"Precious gems, Mr. G."

He observed Patch's condition closely.

"Some attached to the eyes," he continued. "Some to the ears, the navel, other parts of the anatomy. For some unknown reason, this became a tradition that accompanied ownership."

Patch looked down at his drink and realized that there was some kind of drug in it. He tried to stand up, faltered, and shook his head again. He took two unstable steps toward Coulter and fell forward on his knees.

Coulter called sharply, "Justin! Come in here!"

The door to the bedroom opened and the skateboarder came in. There were several suitcases on the bed closed and ready for travel. The youth stood over Patch who was trying to get up. Justin kicked him in the side. Patch winced and fell to the floor, moaning.

"It doesn't look like we'll be needing your help after all, Mr. G," Coulter said coldly. "Another of my operatives is obtaining the Twins all on his own even as we speak."

He put on his hat.

"Good-bye," he said to Patch and nodded to the youth.

As Coulter walked away, Justin kicked Patch in the head, knocking the Apache out cold.

7 Chapter Seven

Somewhere miles and miles to the east, the morning sun glinted off the windshield of the grey Interstate Transport van as it sped along a two lane highway. The driver was humming a tune to himself as Luther napped in the reclined passenger seat. In the back of the van, the armed guard, who was supposed to be protecting the van's precious cargo, also napped.

Without warning, a large truck with the words "Santa Fe Transfer and Storage" painted on it pulled out from a side dirt road onto the highway, completely blocking the van. To avoid hitting the truck, the van driver swerved off the highway towards the side road. But the van was traveling too fast for the driver to be able to control the turn, and the van slid sideways into a ditch.

Immediately the truck backed up until it was even with the van. Two men wearing black ski masks and jump suits exited the truck's cab. Working with rehearsed precision, the masked men swung into action.

Brandishing hand guns, they ran to the van to check the status of its passengers. Neither the driver nor the old man were conscious, but the guard in back was beginning to move around, trying to pull himself together.

Climbing into the van from the driver's side, one of the masked men pointed his gun at the guard. The guard, still not fully functional, reached for his own weapon. The masked man shot him and the guard fell backwards. He didn't move again.

The shooter motioned to his accomplice, and the man ran to the back of the big truck. Opening the doors, he removed a bundle of ropes and gags and brought them back to the van.

Then they dragged the driver out of his seat. He was bleeding from a forehead wound caused by the air bag, but was still alive. They tied and gagged him, carried him around to the back of the van and laid him on the ground.

Opening the back of the van, they found what they were looking for: the crate marked "PROPERTY OF THE ZUNI TRIBE." They unloaded the crate and placed it in the back of their truck.

Quickly, they returned to the van, put the tied-up driver in the back and proceeded to tie and gag the wounded guard. Just then, Luther began to stir and moan. The masked pair pulled him out of the passenger's seat and checked him over. Seeing that he wasn't seriously hurt, they tied and gagged him.

They carried the old man, who was just regaining consciousness, to the back of the truck and placed him inside next to the crate. Just as Luther was opening his eyes, the truck doors closed, leaving him in total darkness.

One of the masked men ran back to the Interstate Transport van and started the engine. He quickly backed it out of the ditch, kicking up dust and dirt. He parked the van about fifty feet from the highway just off the dirt road and locked the doors.

Leaving the bleeding driver and guard behind, the masked men sped off down the highway with both the crate and Luther neatly tucked away in the back.

Back in Santa Fe, Patch began to regain consciousness. He opened his eyes. His head hurt, and the room was dark. Groaning in pain, he lifted himself from the floor and stumbled to the lamp. Fumbling with the switch, he turned it on. He stood there for a moment, one hand on the switch, the other rubbing the back of his neck.

He walked unsteadily through the bedroom and into the bathroom. A quick check in the mirror revealed that his temple was red and swollen.

"That'll teach you to drink gin in the morning," he said to the disheveled man in the mirror.

He turned the water on in the sink and splashed some over his face. Drying himself with a fancy embroidered hotel towel, he stumbled out into the bedroom.

He looked at his watch. Twelve noon.

He began searching the room, turning back the bed covers, removing cushions from the chairs, checking in the drawers, looking for any kind of clue. Finding nothing, he went back into the living room.

He gave the room a quick once-over. Under the cushion of one of the plush chairs, he finally came up with something. It was another one of Kyoto's business cards with the lizard design. Patched turned it over. On the back there is a hand-written name and address: Tribal Antiquities, Inc. 535 Canyon Rd, Santa Fe. Patch grinned as he stumbled out the door.

When he arrived at his office, Patch saw that a light from inside glowed against the glass panel door. He tried the door, but it was locked. That was odd. He took out his keys, quietly unlocked it and slipped in.

He found Jessie asleep on the couch. She stirred and opened her eyes. She sat up and sleepily looked at Patch. Her coat, which was tucked around her legs, fell to the floor.

"Oh, Patch, there you are," she said sleepily. "Did you get the message I left on your cellphone?"

"No, I didn't. Someone removed the battery while I was unconscious at La Posada Hotel."

"What?" said, jumping off the couch.

"Never mind. Why did you call, and why aren't you home with Sykes?"

"She's gone."

Patch sat down on the couch beside her. "Whataya mean she's gone?"

"Just that. When I got up this morning, she had disappeared. There was no sign of her."

As Patch's mind cleared more, a new realization settled in.

"Interesting coincidence," he said. "You sure no one followed you when you took her to your place?"

"Yes, we were very careful." A worried look came over Jessie's face. "Do you think someone got her?" she asked.

"Not unless she wanted them to."

Jessie started to say something, then finally noticed the red lump on Patch's head.

"Your head. What happened?"

She lightly touched the bump and he grimaced.

"I don't know exactly. I went to see Coulter and he put something in my drink. Then one of his goons gave me this little present. I just came to a little while ago."

"You can't go walking around with a bump on your head like that!" Jessie announced.

She reached up to touch his bump again but Patch pulled back.

"It's not as bad as it looks," he lied.

"Patch, this case is getting too dangerous."

"You're probably right, but it's too late to turn back now. What about the couriers? Did Red or Luther phone in their noon progress reports?"

"No. No one's called."

"That's just great," Patch said as he stood. "Everyone remotely related to this case seems to have vanished."

He sighed and stepped away. A light suddenly went on in his mind, and he turned back to Jessie.

"Listen, you stay here and wait for our rez boys to call in."

"Where are you going?" Jessie asked.

"To see an old friend," he replied as he opened the door. "I'm tired of being one step behind on this case."

He winked and slipped out of the office as the door closed behind him.

Western Kansas was no place for two long-haired Indians with rifles and a priceless cargo to be broken down, but that's where Red and Billy were. Twenty miles from nowhere. Deep in the heart of Redneck country. And for some odd reason both of their cellphones stopped working. It wasn't that they didn't have reception. Both phones went totally dead.

Fortunately, they were able to coax the van to a secluded spot away from the highway, away from prying eyes. The van came to rest under a big tree near a creek.

Red had sent Billy hitch-hiking up the highway to see if he could find a phone to call in to Patch and report their situation while he stayed behind to work on the van.

"No luck," Billy said, returning from his unsuccessful venture.

Red slid out from under the front of the van.

"Just suspicious stares from hayseed farmers," Billy continued. "Any luck here?"

"Not yet."

Red opened the van's back doors and hunted for a cloth to wipe his hands. Billy reached in and grabbed a can of soda from their ice chest. He studied the crate as he popped the top on the soda.

"We're really behind schedule," Red said, wiping the grease from his hands. "I bet Geronimo is worried."

"I still wanna know what's in this box that's so all-fired important," Billy said, stroking the side of the crate. "You dragged me way out here in the middle of nowhere, and I don't really even know what for."

"Another tribe's medicine," Red answered with set determination. "You don't want to mess with it, Billy."

"Aw, come on. It won't hurt to take a peek."

He started looking around for the tire iron. "Why don't we pop the lid off?"

Red grabbed Billy's arm.

"Forget it, Billy. We're doing an important job for a friend who helped us out once, so just drop it. Stick to business."

"All right, all right," Billy said begrudgingly. "Don't get so worked up."

"Now go over there and sit down," Red ordered. "I'm almost finished. We'll be back on the road in no time."

Billy sat down by the tree to drink his soda as Red slid back under the engine to complete the repairs. Billy just stared at the crate. Something about its contents had taken a grip on his mind and wouldn't leave him alone.

Minutes later, Red tightened up the last bolt and pulled himself out from under the van.

"All done," he said as he stood up, only to be greeted by the barrel of a rifle.

"Step away from the van." Billy demanded, waving the rifle in Red's face. "I'll take it from here."

Red looked in his friend's eyes. They were clouded, non-focused. It seemed that Billy wasn't really in there.

"Billy, what are you doing?"

"I'm cashing in. I'm tired of being a poor Injun. I figure this precious cargo is my ticket off the rez. I'm sure I can find someone who'll pay a pretty penny for it, whatever it is."

Then Red remembered Patch's warning. He'd said that the contents of the crate supposedly had strange effects on those who spent much time around them.

"Think about what you're doing, man," Red said. "You're not it your right mind right now."

"Shut up and get over there by the tree."

Red took a step away from the van. Billy moved toward the driver's door. As he opened it, he lowered the rifle momentarily. Red made his move.

He dove sideways against the door, bouncing Billy against the door frame. Billy yelled as the rifle dropped, butt first, on the ground discharging one bullet from its barrel. Billy's body jerked back and blood spurted out from somewhere.

"Billy!"

Red leapt to his friend's side, easing his fall to the ground. Billy was unconscious. Red checked him over, discovering that the bullet had pierced Billy in the fat of his upper arm and passed on through the other side.

Seeing that the wound was not fatal, Red retrieved a t-shirt from his overnight bag in the van. He ripped it into strips and wrapped Billy's wounds with them.

Billy regained consciousness and opened his eyes. He looked around. "What happened? How did I get down here?"

"You got a crazy look in your eyes and tried to steal the van," Red replied.

"Huh?" Billy tried to get up. "Ow! What happened to my arm?"

"You don't remember?" Red asked as he helped Billy to his feet.

"No. I don't remember anything."

"We've got to make up for lost time," Red said. "Get in the van, and I'll tell you all about it."

8 Chapter Eight

Patch had maneuvered his vintage motorcycle along Old Santa Fe Trail away from the Plaza towards the collection of museums that stood guard on a hill at the eastern edge of town. A Western Lines tour bus was unloading its human cargo as he roared into the parking lot of the Museum of Indian Arts and Culture on his mechanical steed. The heads of several elderly tourists turned to observe Patch's entrance as if he might be part of some local pageant that was unfolding just for their benefit.

Recognizing their curiosity at seeing an Indian on an Indian motorcycle reminded Patch of one of the many reasons he had a love-hate relationship with Santa Fe. He resented the fact that he, and Native people in general, were considered quaint and colorful relics of a romanticized past. Cowboys and Indians forever locked in contrived historical dance, one not able to exist without the other in America's collective consciousness.

He parked his bike near the entrance of the New Mexico State Anthropology Lab located next to the museum and killed the engine. Hanging his candy apple red helmet over the handle bars, he stepped inside the building.

"Chester Banks," Patch said to the receptionist. "Is he in?"

"Yes, I believe he's downstairs in the archives."

"Could you tell him that I need to see him, please?"

She picked up the phone and dialed. "Chester? There's a man here to see you. His name is..." She looked up at Patch.

"Geronimo." She paused for a moment.

"Uh...he says his name is Geronimo. All right." She hung up. "Down the steps to the right," she said.

Lurking below ground level in a bunker-like enclosure was a repository of artifacts and information that was off limits to tourists and the general public. You had to be a bonafide scholar, researcher, anthropologist or some other brand of rarified intellectual to get a pass to this underworld. Or know somebody who worked there.

"Chester?" Patch called out.

He wove his way through the maze of dusty shelves which contained faded boxes of forgotten files and little pieces of peoples' lives.

"Over here," the old archaeologist's voice rang out through the catacombs. Patch headed for the source of the sound. In a few moments he found the white-haired man peering through a magnifying glass at something on the table.

"What is it today?" Patch asked. "A Folsom point? A Mimbres potshard?"

"Try the tiny metal screw that holds my reading glasses together," Chester replied. "It fell out somewhere around here." As Patch approached to take a look, his eye caught something shiny on the floor.

"Here it is," he said as he stooped to pick it up. He dropped the screw carefully into the grateful man's outstretched hand.

"I guess that's why your business is called Eagle Eye Investigations!" Chester remarked with a smile.

"Good one," Patch said.

He noticed that his old archaeology friend had aged considerably since he'd seen him last.

"Patch," the older man said as he shook the private eye's hand. "How ya been?"

"Can't complain. Nobody listens when I do."

"Complainers never prosper," Chester said. "That's what I always say."

He noticed the lump on Patch's head.

"Did you get the license plate of the truck that hit you?"

"It's worse than it looks," Patch said, rubbing the spot gently. "Listen, Chester, this isn't entirely a social call. I need your help."

"What can an old digger like me do for you?"

"I was hoping you could help me find some information with that high-powered computer of yours."

"You mean the NARDNet?"

"Nerd-net, Nard-net, whatever you call it."

"It's the National Anthropology Resource Database Network."

"Like I said—whatever you call it. I'm trying to put a jigsaw puzzle together, but I don't seem to have all the pieces."

He reached into his pocket, withdrew a piece of paper and handed it to Chester. Patch had scribbled the words "Zuni War Gods" at the top of the paper. Underneath it were the names Ryan Coulter, Sam Kyoto and Kathleen Sykes.

"Anything you could find on these names might be helpful," Patch said. "Do you have time?"

"Does this have anything to do with Willy?"

"It has everything to do with Willy."

"Then I'll make time, but it'll have to wait until later this afternoon. I've got an Anasazi pot that's been laying around for a thousand years which my boss can't wait another hour to get test results on."

"That'll be just fine," Patch chuckled. "Better than fine. That'd be great. I'll have Jessie come by and pick up whatever you find."

Patch headed back towards the stairs.

"The Zuni pieces should be no problem," Chester called after him. "But these people. Who are they? Anthros? Curators? Collectors?"

"Try cut-throat, back-stabbing, black marketeers," Patch replied solemnly, leaving the old man to turn that over in his mind.

Patch steered his motorcycle back through Santa Fe, and then northward on Highway 285 out of town. The stark northern New Mexico landscape sped past him as he hit the 60-mile per hour mark. In his younger years, Johny had often fantasized that his motorcycle was a spirited Apache horse, and that he rode alongside his scavenging Athabascan ancestors across the sagebrush in search of wild game and adventure.

Today, however, he realized he was just another average angst-ridden mortal who had, until this week, succeeded in eluding the legions of demons who had been hovering around the fringes of his life. Now they were closing in on him, fast.

He coaxed the bike's throttle up to 70 mph.

In Pojoaque the highway forked, and he headed west on Highway 502 across the Rio Grande to where it dead-ended at State Highway 30. Turning north, he put the bike on the road to Santa Clara Pueblo and Willie's home.

On the way to Santa Clara, Highway 30 passed through San Ildefonso Pueblo, just west of Black Mesa, the site of Willie's hospital vision of the twin spirits. As he passed by it, Patch looked over at the magnificent flat-topped mountain.

As a kid, Willie had been pumped full of old Pueblo Indian legends by his grandfather about the spirits who supposedly inhabited that mesa. So it made sense, Patch thought, that Willie would dream about this place as he hovered near death in the hospital.

Was it real or was it a delirious hallucination? Patch had accepted it as reality in the rush of relief that accompanied the news that Willie was going to survive. At the time, Patch was convinced that Willie's knowledge of Abe's request for help was proof that these spirits were real. The door into "Indian superstitions" that Patch had shut so tightly long-ago momentarily sprang open.

But now, in the cold hard light of rational thought and in the face the sudden disappearance of anyone or anything related to the War Gods, Patch was prepared to close the door once again. It served him right for being almost seduced into belief.

As he neared Santa Clara, the traffic became thicker, which was typical on a Pueblo Feast Day. Friends and relatives of Pueblo residents, along with carloads of gawking tourists, poured into the reservation to experience the festivities, taste the food, hear the sounds and watch the dances.

Tribal police herded cars into a field near the village that had been converted into a parking lot for the day. Patch pulled his bike up to an empty spot along an adobe wall that skirted the village. After he killed the engine, he could hear the familiar rhythmic chanting and drumming that accompanied the Corn Dance.

He joined the flow of visitors streaming into the Plaza and headed for the Chino home, which occupied a corner spot on the north side of the Plaza. Pueblo Indian arts and crafts booths had been laid out in grids that occupied every spare inch space in the dirt streets of the village. Patch wove his way through the browsers and the buyers as quickly as he could.

Soon he reached Willy and Rachel's family home, an ancient adobe dwelling set shoulder-to-shoulder with several others in this row. He stuck his head in the door to see how crowded it was. As was usual on a Feast Day, several guests waited patiently in the living room for their turn at the dining table. Pueblo women often spent several days cooking and storing food in preparation for the annual event and the crowds who would pour through their homes.

The Apache stepped through the living room and into the kitchen-dining room where several apron-clad women bustled about. Patch saw Willy's mom, one of Willy's aunts and a cousin who were in various stages of preparing and serving meals. Seated around a long table in the center of the room were about a dozen guests avidly focused on eating and talking. Rachel's husband, Walter, was among them.

Patch entered the room just as Rachel stepped in through a side door from the storeroom. She was carrying a large cooking pot. Her eyes met his, but she quickly looked away to avoid revealing any signs of their illicit intimacy.

"Mom, look who's here," Rachel said as she placed the pot on the stove. She pointed toward Patch with her lips. Rachel's mother turned around. So did Walter.

"Geronimo!" Mrs. Chino said enthusiastically. "I'm so glad you could come."

Drying her hands on her apron, she glided across the kitchen floor to give him a welcoming hug.

"Isn't it wonderful how quickly Willy is recovering?"

"Yes it is, Mrs. Chino," Patch said sincerely. "He's very lucky."

"Luck had nothing to do with it, young man," she said sternly. "I've been praying day and night for his recovery. God has seen fit to answer my prayers. It wouldn't hurt you to do a little more praying and a little less partying, Geronimo."

"Yes, ma'am. You're probably right."

Patch sometimes uncontrollably reverted to a twelve year old in Mrs. Chino's presence. She seemed to carry the universal authority of a woman who acted as everyone's mother.

An Anglo woman got up from the dinner table and approached Mrs. Chino.

"Thank you for a wonderful meal," the guest said. "The green chile was especially good this year."

"I'm glad you liked it," Mrs. Chino replied. "Please have a seat out there in the living room, and I'll come out and visit in a just a minute."

The woman exited the kitchen. Mrs. Chino led Patch over to the place the woman had just vacated at the table.

"Sit down and I'll bring you a plate and a bowl of posole," she said."You have to stay and eat."

Patch did as he was told and then looked across the table and directly into Rachel's eyes. She looked away. He looked at Walter who was sitting next to her.

"Hello, Walter," Patch said calmly. "How have you been?"

"Busy," the older Anglo man said as Mrs. Chino brought the food and some silverware. "How 'bout yourself?"

"Same here," Patch said with a sideways glance to Rachel.

"What's the matter, Rachel? Aren't you going to speak to me?"

She shifted uncomfortably in her chair.

"Hello, Patch," she responded with a tinge of annoyance in her voice.

The Apache inwardly delighted in her discomfort, forced to sit across from her lover and beside her husband.

He began serving himself generous portions of everything in sight: red chile posole, oven bread, pork tamales, potato salad and corn. These were the makings of a perfect Pueblo meal.

After taking a few bites from his plate, Patch looked up at his lover's husband.

"Walter," he said, "You're just the man I wanted to see."

Rachel gasped ever so slightly, then pretended to choke on a bite of food.

"Oh?" the man answered. "And what could you possibly want with me?"

"You know I'm working on a very serious case, trying to find out who shot Willy and why."

"Of course," he replied. "Anything I can do to help."

"You're a member of this Tribal Antiquities group that's meeting in Santa Fe next week, aren't you?"

"That's right."

"Ever heard of a guy by the name of Ryan Coulter?"

"Of course," Walter said. "He's one of the heavyweights in the business. He's got connections all over the world."

Patch chuckled.

"One of the heavyweights. That's funny. The man can hardly get up out of his chair."

"So you've met him?"

"Briefly. He's definitely linked to Willy's shooting and verifiably engaged in the illegal buying and selling of American Indian religious icons."

"I knew you were reckless, John, but I didn't think you were foolish. Those are very serious charges that could ruin a long and respected career, if you're not careful."

Patch looked at Rachel, then back at Walter.

"How did you ever get mixed up with this guy, Rachel? Beneath this veil of dignified respectability beats the heart of a cultural predator."

Abruptly, Patch pushed his chair back from the table and got up. Walking towards Willy's mom who was working at the stove, he said, "Thanks for the great food, Mrs. Chino, but I just realized what time it is. I have to be back in Santa Fe to meet with someone."

She hugged him.

"I will pray for you, Geronimo," she said tenderly. "Don't worry. Everything will be all right."

He smiled and kissed her lightly on the forehead and left.

The sun was climbing down out of the sky as Patch made his way back to Santa Fe. He tuned out the road in front of him as his mind replayed some old tapes.

Rachel was the first girl Patch ever kissed. Even in the strict boarding school setting, it hadn't been that hard to sneak off into the trees behind the gym for a little experimentation with the opposite sex. Willy kept watch to make sure they weren't caught.

Sure, there'd been plenty of girls to experiment with in Patch's life, but he'd always kept fond nostalgic memories of Rachel because she had been the first. What he hadn't realized until it was too late is that she was the one. His own cynical, self-protective ego hadn't allowed him to ever tell her how he felt, and seeing his tendency to play around, she had looked elsewhere for stability and loyalty in her life.

So it was with bitter-sweet delight that Patch had welcomed Rachel back into his arms when she went searching for the passion and sense of personal identity that was missing in her marriage.

Sure, the current arrangement allowed him to still fool around with other women. But he was realizing that it was a mistake. That arrangement was feeling more and more hollow with every passing day. Deep down inside, in a place hidden most of the time, he knew that the hole in his heart and his gut he tried to fill with booze and sex was a hole that only Rachel could fill.

Having her, yet not having her, was proving all too painful. Gathering the courage to tell her–that was the task.

9 Chapter Nine

In Santa Fe, Patch turned on Guadalupe Street, followed the road past the cemetery and made a bee-line for the El Dorado Hotel. Inside the hotel, he paused to call his office. As the phone rang, he noticed that Jake, the hotel detective, was putting the make on the girl behind the registration desk.

"Eagle Eye," Jessie answered.

"It's me. Did Red call in?"

"Yeah, finally. He said he ran into some trouble on the road, but that everything was fine now."

"Trouble? What kind of trouble?"

"He said he'd fill you in when he got here. He had to call from a pay phone."

"A pay phone? I didn't know those still existed outside Santa Fe. And the decoy team?"

"Nothing."

"Call Interstate Transport and tell them what's up. Have them trace the route and see if they can find them. I hope Luther's all right. What about Chester at the Anthro Lab? Did he come up with anything for us?"

"I've got an envelope from him right here," Jessie replied. "He told me to tell you that Coulter, interestingly enough, had just closed down his New York office and is having all his mail forwarded to Paris."

"As in France?"

"As in France."

"So the fat man's clearing out. Thanks, sweetie. If you haven't already, take a break to get some dinner. But get right back to the office in case something else develops. I'll see you in a little while."

He clicked off the call, tip-toed quietly across the terrazo tiles. Sneaking up behind Jake, Patch tapped him on the shoulder.

"Evening, Jake," he said. "Hard at work as usual."

Jake turned and smiled. "Hello, Patch. What brings you back so soon?"

"I need a favor," the Apache replied.

The girl Jake had been talking to said, "I'll see you later, Jake," and walked away. Patch could see Jake's disappointment in this turn of events. But the house detective shook it off.

"Name it," Jake replied.

"You got a guest named Kyoto."

"That Japanese fella you were talking to."

Patch walked Jake toward the elevators. "What's the chance you'd let me in to search his room?"

"Better than average," Jake said without a second thought. "Let's go."

Upstairs, Jake knocked at Kyoto's room. When there was no answer, he unlocked the door and the pair entered. Everything, including the lizard in its cage, was still in place. Patch and Jake neatly rummaged through everything in the room.

"What exactly are we looking for?" Jake asked.

"Signs of recent travel or plans for future travel. But any hint of anything could be useful right now."

Then Patch spied something across the room on the phone table. The Santa Fe phone book lay open. Patch practically jumped at it. The book was open to the yellow page section titled "Moving and Storage." There was a half-page ad for the Santa Fe Transfer and Storage Company. It had been marked and highlighted.

"I think I've found the hint I was looking for," Patch said, showing the ad to Jake. Patch noted the company's address and they left the room.

Patch rode his motorcycle southward down Cerrillos Road through the night towards the Santa Fe Industrial Park. As he turned off Cerrillos onto Airport Road, he noticed an orange glow in the night sky up ahead. Turning into the Industrial Park, his headlight caught the park's directory, which placed the Santa Fe Transfer and Storage company in space number fourteen.

He rounded the circular road leading through the park until the building came into sight. What he saw stopped him dead in his tracks. The warehouse was engulfed in flames. Fire trucks and police cars swarmed the area.

Sizing up the situation, Patch headed for an ambulance parked near the burning building. A couple of firemen raced past him headed for their truck as he parked his bike.

An older man was seated on the back end of the ambulance being checked over by a couple of medics. As he approached the ambulance, one of the medics stepped toward him.

Patch flashed his private investigator license at the guy.

"Quite a bonfire," Patch said. "When did this all start?"

"We got the call about half an hour ago," the medic replied.

"Anybody hurt?"

"Only Mr. Jenkins here. He was the only one on duty at the time."

"Can I talk to him?"

"Sure. He got a bump on the head and inhaled a little smoke. He'll be all right."

Patch approached Jenkins. "What happened here?"

"I'm not sure," Jenkins replied. "Who are you?"

"I'm a local private investigator, and I'm afraid something belonging to one of my clients might be in that fire. Did you see anything before this started?"

"One of our trucks came in a little while ago from a long distance haul," Jenkins explained. "I went around to the loading dock to see what they'd brought in. As I rounded the corner to take a look, I was whacked in the head from behind."

He touched the bump on his head. It reminded Patch of his own bump.

"When I came to," Jenkins continued, "the place was in flames. The drivers had disappeared. That's the truck they were driving over there."

"Mind if I take a look inside the back?" Patch asked.

"Go ahead. I don't see how it could hurt. It's empty."

Patch retrieved a flashlight from one of the saddle bags on his bike. Opening the large back doors of the truck, he shined the light inside.

The light caught something in the corner. He pulled himself up and into the cargo area. Shining the light along the floor, he walked over to the object and squatted down to take a closer look.

It turned out to be a small leather pouch, closed at the top with a draw-string. Picking it up, Patch opened the pouch and reached in with two fingers. He took a pinch of the contents out and held his fingers up to the light for close examination. A yellow powdery substance clung to his fingertips. He touched the powder to his tongue.

"Corn pollen," he said to himself. "Luther was in here."

He closed the bag and put it in his pocket. He climbed down out of the truck, closed the doors and jumped on his bike. He waved to Mr. Jenkins as he sped off into the night.

When he arrived back at his office, Jessie was waiting in Patch's leather chair. He sat on his desk and handed her the leather pouch.

"This must've belonged to Luther," Patch declared. "I figure he's been kidnapped along with the decoy War Gods."

"The Interstate Transport guards finally reported back to St. Louis," Jessie said. "One of them had been shot by whoever hijacked the van and stole the fakes."

"Somebody's going to be pissed when they find out all they got was two old logs. What did Chester find?"

She handed over a manila envelope. Patch opened it, and pulled out two computer print-outs. At the top were the words "Search Results: Ryan Coulter." Below it was a brief bio along with an even briefer report.

"Suspected of trading in black market antiquities, though never indicted," the report read. Coulter's New York address was printed below that. Chester had written a note in pencil beside the address.

"I found that this office was closed as of August 1. All inquiries are to be forwarded to 323 Rue de la Rouge; Paris, FRANCE."

At the top of the second page, Patch read "Search Results: Kathleen Sykes." A short bio followed, which pretty much verified what Kathleen had already told Patch. Below it, however, was a new piece of information.

"Married to international investor and art collector Payton Sykes of San Francisco. Sykes is suspected of trading in black market art forgeries, though never convicted."

"Pretty unsavory characters we're dealing with," Patch said, dropping the papers on his desk. "What do you think of all this?"

"I think it's really exciting," Jessie said with almost bubbly delight. "Stolen artifacts, Willy's vision, and now a kidnapped medicine man. This is a lot more interesting than your usual cases."

"And a lot more dangerous," Patch reminded her solemnly. "I expected Luther to bring the decoys here when they arrived in town, but now I'm afraid of what might have happened to him."

This sobering thought eliminated Jessie's giddiness.

Just then they heard the outer office door opening and closing. Patch sat up straight in his chair, waiting, listening. He motioned for her to wait there. Walking to his office door, he opened it and peered out.

Luther was leaning with his back against the closed outer office door. His shirt was torn. His face was pale and smudged.

"My god! Luther!" Patch exclaimed.

"Abe said—" He tried to speak but was having trouble breathing. A bubbling sound started in his throat, choking his words. Then he fell forward.

Patch rushed across the room just in time to break his fall. He gently eased the Indian elder to the floor.

Jessie entered the room, and seeing the old man's condition, froze in her tracks. Patch withdrew his hand from Luther's back. It was covered with blood. Jessie gasped. Then her boss lifted the old man and placed him on the couch.

"Jessie, bring me a towel, and call 911. We need an ambulance here quick."

Jessie, still frozen in place, did not respond.

"Jessie, snap out of it. Do like I tell you."

Jessie blinked her eyes and started to move. After handing Patch a towel, she made the call. Patch wiped the blood off his hands and began applying pressure to the wound.

"I'm at number 76 San Francisco, upstairs," Jessie said to the dispatcher. "We need an ambulance. An elderly gentleman just entered our office and he's been hurt bad."

She looked at Luther.

"Yeah, Eagle Eye Investigations," she continued. "Please hurry."

She hung up and went back to Patch.

"Is he going to be all right?" she asked.

"I don't know. Get another towel and apply pressure to the wound to stop the bleeding."

Just then the phone rang. Patch answered as Jessie tended to Luther's wound.

"Red," Patch said. "Man, am I glad to hear from you. Where are you?"

"At the Quick Mart across from the National Cemetery," Red said.

"Good. Don't come here. It's too risky. Meet me in the alley behind St. Francis Cathedral. You know where that is?"

"Yeah, I know the place."

"Keep out of sight. I'll see you in ten minutes."

Patch hung up.

"Shouldn't we call Abe?' Jessie asked.

"Later. First take care of Luther. I've got to meet the rez boys to get the statues." As he opened the door, he looked at Jessie. She was a little panicked.

"It'll be all right, sister," he said. "We'll get through this."

She sighed, then smiled at him and nodded. He headed out the door and down the stairs.

After he left, the phone rang again. Reluctantly, Jessie answered.

"Hello... Kathleen! It's you. No, he just left. Where are you?... Yes, I got it."

As she wrote down the address, the phone went dead.

"Hello. Hello," Jessie said fearfully. She hung up and ripped the notepaper from the pad.

Checking Luther quickly, Jessie bolted down the stairs to catch Patch.

She reached Patch in the alley just as he kicked-started his bike.

"Patch" she yelled over the roar of the engine. "Patch!"

He looked up at her.

"What is it?" he shouted.

"The mystery woman called!"

"What?"

"Kathleen."

Jessie reached over and turned the engine off.

"What did you do that for?" Patch asked.

"Kathleen called. She's being held hostage!"

"Well, why didn't you say so?"

She glared at him for a moment.

"Just kidding. Where is she?"

"Five-thirty-five Canyon Road," Jessie replied. "She sounded scared, but it could be a trap. The line went dead before she finished telling me what was going on."

"I know that address. It's the one hand written on the back of Kyoto's card. But I've got to get the statues first."

He thought for a minute.

"Call Abe. Tell him what happened to Luther. But don't say anything to anyone about the Twins. Got that?"

"Yeah, I got it. Just get going. And be careful."

"Anything for you, babe."

He smiled and started the engine again.

"Remind me to give you a raise when this is all over," he said and sped off down the alley.

Jessie watched him leave as she slowly climbed back up the stairs.

Patch rode the short block to St. Francis Cathedral and parked his bike in the back alley beside a low stone wall. He checked to see if anyone had followed him. All clear.

A moment later, Red and Billy stepped out of the shadows. Patch smiled when he saw them. The smile faded when he saw the bandage on Billy's arm.

"Don't ask, man," Red said before Patch could speak. "Just get this Zuni medicine away from us so we can go back to Mescalero. We have to get our own medicine man to smudge us off as soon as possible."

"Where are the statues?"

"Still in the van," Red said. "I don't want to touch 'em."

Patch followed them to the parked van. The crate lay open in the back.

He reached in and picked up the black bag. It was bulky but surprisingly light for its size. He stepped out of the van, and Red shut the doors.

"Now we're even," he said and climbed in behind the wheel. "I'll talk to you after I'm sure these spirits aren't going to mess with us any more," he added as he started the engine.

Patch knew better than to probe this any farther with Red. They'd been in and out of trouble together through the years, and Patch had learned to recognize when his friend needed space.

"Thanks, for doing this," Patch said as Red pulled away.

Carrying the bag, Patch approached a side door of the cathedral. With a knock and a short wait, the door opened. A sleepy, red-faced man in a nightshirt opened the door, yawning and scratching his head. The man instantly recognized Patch.

"Geronimo?" the man said with a thick Irish accent. "Do you know what time it is?"

"Yes, Father O'Malley. I'm sorry to wake you, but I have an emergency."

"Always with the emergencies. I'm a priest, not an ambulance driver. What is it this time?"

"Can you hold on to this for me? It's important that it's kept safe and quietly tucked away until Jessie or I come for it."

"Of course, I'll look after it for you, but only because I promised your mother that I'd keep an eye on you. What is it?"

"It's better that you don't know for now. I'll explain it all later."

The priest's relunctance to get involved showed on his face.

"Don't worry. It's nothing illegal."

"Well, that's a relief," the padre said.

"Thanks, Father. You're the best. I owe you."

Patch placed the large bag in the priest's waiting arms and turned to leave.

"Well, it wouldn't hurt you to stop in for mass some morning. It'd mean a lot to your mother."

Walking away, Patch said, "I will, Father. Real soon. I promise."

The priest shook his head, knowing that Patch wouldn't keep this promise. He looked down curiously at the mysterious black bag as he closed the door.

Patch headed slowly up the narrow, gallery-lined Canyon Road. The bike's headlight illuminated various old adobe structures and gallery signs as it moved along.

When he reached the five hundred block, Patch pulled the bike over to the side of the road and killed the engine. He parked it in a narrow alleyway just off the road and out of sight.

Quietly the private eye walked up the sidewalk checking out the addresses. He came to number five-thirty-five. It was an old adobe art gallery surrounded by a low adobe wall. Hanging on the front exterior of the building was a banner that read: THE FUTURE HOME OF TRIBAL ANTIQUITIES, INC. There was a light coming through a rear side window.

Creeping up to the window, Patch peered inside. In the center of the room sat a large wooden crate with the words PROPERTY OF THE ZUNI TRIBE stenciled on the side. It was open and empty.

He heard footsteps approaching from another part of the gallery and ducked down. After a moment, he cautiously peered through the window again.

Two men had entered the room. One was wearing a Santa Fe Transfer and Storage jumpsuit. The other, a broad-shouldered goon of a guy, wore a suit and tie. They walked to the open crate. The man in the suit bent down and picked up some of the packing material from inside the crate.

"You really botched it this time," he said to the one in the jump suit. "Coulter will be here any minute and he's most unhappy."

The Suit threw the packing material in the other man's face and punched him in the jaw, knocking him into the crate. Using a wad of rope from the floor, the Suit tied up the unconscious man where he lay.

Patch continued to watch the action from outside. Just then he heard the sound of a gun being cocked near his ear. Patch turned and came face to face with the barrel of a forty-five. He looked up to see Coulter's pretty boy assistant, Justin, holding the gun.

"Nice view from down there?" Justin asked.

Patch stood up and turned toward him.

"You've just been itchin' to use that thing on me. Why don't you go ahead and pull the trigger? Then we'll see how your boss likes it."

"You've got a smart mouth on you, mister. Come on, you can see everything better from inside."

Justin stuck the gun in Patch's side prodding him to move. Patch and the skateboarder entered the dark front room of the gallery. A moment later a light came on revealing Coulter and Kyoto standing on either side of Kathleen. Kyoto held her by the arm displaying his pistol. No words were spoken. In another moment the Suit came into the room from the rear of the gallery.

"Well, well, well, how convenient," Coulter said sarcastically. "We're all here, aren't we? Let's go in, sit down, get comfortable and talk. Shall we?"

Coulter was ever so polite.

"Whatever you say," Patch responded dryly. "You're holding all the guns."

Kyoto pushed Kathleen toward Patch. Coulter led the group into the adjoining room. Justin nudged Patch in the same direction with his gun.

The group entered the gallery's front sitting room. Patch escorted Kathleen to a sofa by the window and sat down with her. She clung to him in fear, and he let her. Coulter lowered his large body into a padded rocking chair. Kyoto chose an armchair by the window, placing his pistol on a nearby table. The Suit leaned against the wall near Coulter. Justin remained standing near the doorway.

"So here we are," Patch said. "One big happy family. But we haven't all been properly introduced. Who's the suit?"

"This is Braxton, one of my buyers. He's been busy elsewhere for several days."

"Did you enjoy that little sleep you had yesterday?" Braxton asked.

"Oh, yeah, I had pleasant dreams," Patch replied. "But let's get down to business."

He turned to Coulter.

"Are ready to make the first payment and take delivery of the Twins?"

Kathleen sat up straight with a look of surprise. Patch patted her on the knee, but kept his gaze fixed on Coulter.

"As a matter of fact I am. All my attempts at retrieving the statues having failed."

He gave his team a disgusted look. Then he took an envelope from his coat pocket, turned it over for a moment studying it. He pitched it, spinning sideways, to Patch.

"It seems I am in your debt, Mr.G."

Patch caught the envelope, opened it and removed a stack of stiff new one thousand dollar bills. He spread them and counted them.

"Ten thousand?" Patch said it as a question. "I'm very disappointed. We talked about a much higher figure."

"That was talk," Coulter replied. "This is cold har cash. A bird in hand, and all that. And there are more of us now to split the take."

Patch re-aligned the bills into a neat stack, returned them to the envelope and tucked the flap over them. He placed the envelope on the arm of the sofa.

"That may be, but I'm still the one holding the Twins."

"Need I remind you that even though you have the Twins, we have you?" Braxton bragged.

"That doesn't worry me too much, right now, but we can come back to the money later," Patch replied.

Leaving the envelope on the arm of the sofa, Patch stood up and began pacing.

"There's another issue we've got to take care of first," he continued. "Who's gonna be the fall guy for this whole damn mess?"

Coulter's eyebrow curled.

"Fall guy?" he asked.

"You know," Patch explained. "Somebody to hang the shootings on."

"Shooting, Mr. Geronimo," clarified Kyoto. "Morgan undoubtedly shot your partner."

"That may be your theory, but I've got my own. But, we've got to give the police—."

Coulter interrupted.

"Come now Mr. G. You can't expect us to believe that you can't handle a little—."

Patch interrupted back.

"I'm up to my neck in quicksand over this thing, Coulter. I've got to have somebody to hand over to the D.A. when the time comes, or I'm it."

He nodded toward Justin.

"What about this punk here? He did shoot Morgan, didn't he?"

After a pregnant pause, Coulter laughed heartily.

"You are quite a character, Mr. G. I must admit. But it's preposterous. The very idea. I think of Justin as my own son."

Pausing and becoming more serious, Coulter continued.

"Anyway, what would keep him from telling the police every last detail about us and the Twins?"

Patch returned to the sofa and sat down next to Kathleen.

"He could talk all he wants," Patch replied. "Nobody'd believe him. They'd just think he was trying to save his own neck."

Coulter laughed again, then turned and looked at Justin.

"What do you think, my boy. Pretty funny, isn't it?"

Justin took a few threatening steps towards Patch.

"Hilarious," he said. "Ha, ha. Make him lay off me, Mr. Coulter."

Coulter waved Justin back.

"Suppose we give them you, Mr. G, or Ms. Sykes, here? How about that?"

"Have you forgotten the position you're in?" Patch reminded him. "You want the Twins. I've got them. A fall guy is part of my asking price."

Keeping his eyes cool and steady on Coulter, Patch patted Kathleen on the knee again.

Coulter cleared his throat.

"Well, sir, if you're really serious about this, I suppose we ought to at least hear you out. How would you be able to fix it so Justin couldn't do us any harm?"

Justin became alarmed.

"Our district attorney is like most," Patch began. "To get a clean conviction on one man, she'll let a whole gaggle of equally guilty accomplices go free."

"Trying to gather all of us up and convict us will be a lengthy, tangled process. If she's got Justin here, it's all neatly wrapped up."

Justin couldn't take any more. He lunged for Patch.

"I said lay off. I've had just about enough of you!"

Patch stood up to repulse Justin's charge. They locked arms in struggle. Coulter nodded to Braxton to step in. Braxton pulled out his pistol and rushed to the pair. He came up behind Justin and whacked him in the back of the head with the butt of the pistol. Justin grunted and fell to the floor, out cold.

Coulter was displeased with the whole turn of events, but Patch had him over a barrel.

"Mr. G, you drive a hard bargain, but I see that I must accept your offer."

Patch and Braxton picked up Justin by the feet and shoulders. Kathleen got up from the sofa and moved away, picking up the envelope full of money as she rose. That move hadn't escaped Patch.

They laid the knocked-out youth on the sofa. Kyoto sat down on the sofa near the boy's head. He stroked his face protectively, almost affectionately, and moved the hair from his eyes.

"Well, now that that's settled, I can get the Twins for you come daylight," Patch reported.

"All right, but in the meantime, I think we should all stay in each other's sight until our business has been finished," Coulter said, looking toward the sofa. "And the envelope?"

"Ms. Sykes has it," Patch said.

"Yes, yes, I do," Kathleen said, a little surprised. She patted the side pocket of her jacket. "Right here where it's safe."

"Well, hang on to it nice and tight," Patch told her, "at least for the time being."

Patch found a new place to sit.

"So I'll make a call in a little while, and have the Twins delivered here."

He pulled out his rolling paper and tobacco and began rolling a cigarette.

"We've got some time to kill," he said. "Why don't you fill me in on some of the missing details? I find this whole affair fascinating."

Coulter pondered the question a moment, then decided he had nothing to lose.

"As I'm sure you know, Mr. G, Morgan was Ms. Sykes partner in a short-lived attempt to recover the Twins for their own gain. We believed that dealing with Morgan as we did would cause Ms. Sykes to re-think her plan."

"Don't you think murdering Morgan was a little harsh," Patch asked, "as far as sending think-it-over messages go?"

"We had tried to reason with Morgan before," Coulter replied. "We gave it one last try that night, but he was determined to stick to the plan he and Ms. Sykes had cooked up. So Justin followed him back to his hotel and did what he had to do."

"And what about yesterday morning? You said one of your operatives was in possession of the Twins, just before I took my little nap."

Patch touched the sore spot on his head.

"Braxton had arranged for the Twins to be re-directed on their way to Santa Fe and brought to a pre-arranged location."

"Santa Fe Transfer and Storage," Patch said.

"So at that point there seemed to be no more need of your services. Kyoto and I went down to the warehouse to meet Braxton and retrieve the Twins, but Ms. Sykes and her partner had beat us there."

"Ah, yes, her silent partner," Patch interjected. "Payton Sykes. I've heard about him."

He looked at Kathleen who was surprised at this revelation. He turned back to Coulter.

"But you were saying about the warehouse?"

"By the time we got there, the Twins were already gone," Coulter continued. "Sykes made off with both the Twins and the medicine man. Slipped right through our fingers."

He looked at Kathleen.

"And so all we found was her and an empty crate," the chubby man added.

"Too bad for Kathleen that her hubby decided to keep the Twins all to himself," Kyoto said. "When we got there, she was tied and gagged beside the empty crate. And boy was she pissed."

"I told you!" Kathleen proclaimed, jumping to her feet. "That crate was empty when we got there."

"You can tell when she's lying, Mr. G," Coulter said sarcastically. "Her lips are moving."

"So you torched the warehouse before you left?" Patch said.

"That's a rather embarrassing point," Braxton replied. It seems that Justin, among his many other traits, is a pyromaniac. He was so angry that the Twins weren't there, he set fire to the place."

At that moment, Justin groaned and rolled over on his side. He opened his eyes and blinked a couple of times.

"I'm afraid you'll have to get the rest of the story from Ms. Sykes," Coulter said.

Justin sat up and looked around, trying to orient himself. His eyes locked on Patch, and he remembered what he was doing before he had been knocked out. He lunged for Patch once again. Once again, Braxton responded. He pounced on Justin's back and pinned his arms behind him. Justin struggled to see who had him.

"Hey, what's going on here?" Justin demanded.

"Justin, I'm truly sorry to be losing you, and I want you to know that I think of you as my own son," Coulter explained sympathetically. "But sometimes in life you must make sacrifices. Take him in back and tie him up with the other fellow for now." Thinking out loud, Coulter said, "So many loose ends."

"You got any coffee in this place?" Patch asked.

"There should be some in the kitchen," Braxton replied.

"Good," Patch said. "We're gonna need a pot."

He turned to Kathleen.

"I don't suppose you're really the domestic type, but would you mind going in the kitchen and whipping us up a pot of coffee?"

Kathleen started for the kitchen without comment.

"Oh, you'd better leave that envelope with me," Patch added.

She stopped dead in her tracks, slowly retraced a couple of steps and handed him the envelope. She shot him a daggered look, then marched for the kitchen.

Patch continued his little inquest.

"Back to the original subject: money. Ten thousand is a little insulting, don't you think?"

"I only offered you five," Kyoto said. "You seemed fine with that amount at the time."

"Yeah, but that was a few days ago. Times have changed. Inflation and what-not."

'Mr. G, I assure you on my word as a gentleman that if I had more to give you, I would," Coulter replied. "But that's all I have or can raise at the moment."

"All right then. I guess I'll have to take your word for it."

"Let me offer you a word of advice, free of charge," Coulter whispered.

"And what would that be?" Patch asked suspiciously.

Coulter nodded toward the kitchen.

"Be careful with that one."

"Dangerous?"

"Extremely."

"Thanks for the tip," Patch replied coolly.

He called toward the kitchen.

"How's the coffee coming?"

"Keep your shirt on. It's coming," Kathleen replied.

Coulter looked at his watch.

"It's six am. May we get started?"

"Oh, sure, sure."

Patch pulled out his cellphone and dialed a number. While he waited for a response, he hummed the theme from "Mission: Impossible" to himself.

Finally, his call was answered.

"Hello, Jessie," Patch said. "Rise and shine, doll. I need you to run a very important errand."

"Go see Father O'Malley and retrieve the items I gave him for safe-keeping. That's right. Bring them to me A.S.A.P. I'm at the address Kathleen gave over the phone. Oh, and hustle, will ya, hun? Bye."

As Patch finished the call, Kathleen brought a tray with coffee and cups from the kitchen. She took the tray to Patch. He gave her an uneasy grin as he poured himself a cup. As she walked away to take coffee to the others, the grin disappeared.

10 Chapter Ten

An hour passed. Golden morning light had begun to stream into the room through open curtains at one of the windows. Coulter read a newspaper. Kyoto typed on his laptop computer. Braxton slouched in a chair. Patch drank more coffee and smoked a cigarette. Kathleen was curled up in an overstuffed chair with her eyes wide open.

A loud knock came at the door. Rising from his chair, Patch looked toward the door.

"That must be our package now," Coulter said. "Shall we go to the door together, Mr. G?"

"By all means," Patch replied politely.

Patch opened the door to find Jessie standing there struggling to hold the bulky black bag. She looked nervously at Patch who smiled back calmly. He took the bag from her.

"Thanks a million, dear," he said calmly. "You're a real life saver."

"Be careful, Patch," she said. "Are you all right?"

"Me? I'm fine," he reassured her. "Don't worry about me. I'm turning over a new leaf. I even promised Father O'Malley I'd go to mass one morning. Now you'd better run along. See you later at the office."

He winked and smiled again. She turned and walked away as he closed the door.

Patch carried the bag into the front gallery room across from the sitting room where they'd been waiting. Several antique Native American artifacts were displayed in cases around the room.

He placed the bag on an empty table in the center of the room.

"And there's your Twins, just like I promised," he said. "Not much to look at really. Except for those gems stuck all over them."

"And the big unsolved mystery is just how did you get them from Payton Sykes?" Kyoto asked suspiciously.

"I didn't," Patch answered. "Because he never had them. What Braxton here hijacked, and Payton, in turn intercepted, were fakes. Decoys. Smoke and mirrors."

Kathleen was dumbstruck, but silent.

"Very resourceful, Johnny," Sykes commented. "I can see I underestimated you."

"Shall we?" Kyoto motioned towards the bag. Everyone converged on the table, anticipating a look at the notorious Twins. Coulter opened the top of the bag and peaked inside.

"Finally, after all these years," he said with glazed eyes. He pulled one of the statues out and handed it to Kyoto. There was the rather plain, weathered, wooden statue covered with strategically placed jewels.

"Ah, how exquisite in it's simplicity," Kyoto remarked. He put it on the table as Coulter withdrew the other one from the bag. He placed it beside the first. Then he nodded to Kyoto.

Kyoto pulled up a chair and sat down at the table. Then he took a jeweler's glass and small tool kit out of his side coat pocket. Pulling one of the statues close to him, he opened his tool kit.

He used a pair of small needle nose pliers from the kit and carefully peeled back the prongs of one of the gem settings. He then retrieved a pair of tweezers from the kit and gently removed the gem from it's setting.

Putting the jeweler's glass to his eye, he tried to examine the stone, but realized there was not enough light. He looked toward the window and, seeing sunlight streaming in, moved to the window. He carefully examined the stone for a moment.

Everyone in the room held their breath.

Then Kyoto removed the jeweler's glass from his eye and turned to Coulter.

"It's a fake," he said disappointedly.

"Are you sure?" Coulter demanded.

"Of course I'm sure," Kyoto snapped. "Don't you think I know my business? It's nothing but a piece of glass."

He dropped it on the floor and crushed it under foot like it was a cigarette butt.

"That's wild," Patch chuckled. "You've been chasing after two worthless pieces of wood covered with costume jewelry all this time."

"All right, Mr. G," Coulter barked. "You've had your fun. What did you do with the real Twins or the real jewels?"

"I hate to disappoint you, but those are the only Twins I know anything about. They came straight from the medicine man's hands."

He squinted at Kathleen.

"If anybody did any switching, it was somebody else."

"No, Patch. I don't know anything about it. I swear!"

Payton must've gotten the real ones somehow, and pretended they had been stolen so he wouldn't have to share them with me!"

"Poor baby," Patch taunted. "Double-crossed by a better double-crosser."

"This whole operation is a complete farce," Kyoto screamed at Coulter. "I don't know why I ever agreed to collaborate with you. You fucking asshole."

He moved toward Coulter. Braxton stepped in to block him.

"Now don't be like that, Kyoto," Coulter said with his usual politeness. "What do you want to do? Stand around crying and calling each other names, or shall we go after Sykes while the trail is still fresh?"

Kyoto relaxed.

"I don't think I could stand any more disappointments," he said.

"Oh, come now. I've been after the Twins for the last five years. If I spend a little longer on the search, no matter."

Kyoto mulled it over for a moment as he began putting away his jeweler's tools.

"Braxton, would you mind fetching Justin from the back room, please?" Coulter requested politely. Braxton nodded and exited.

"Well, Mr. Kyoto," Coulter continued. "What's it going to be?"

"Okay. I'll stick with you a little longer, Coulter," Kyoto replied. "But there'd better not be any more foul-ups."

He picked up his pistol and pointed it at Patch. "But what do we do with them?"

"Leave them to their own devices, unless... Mr. G, you're a resourceful man. It might be interesting to have you along on the hunt."

"Thanks. I'm flattered, but I'll make out all right here."

"Suit yourself. But I will have to ask you for the return of that envelope," Coulter said, extending his hand.

"I came through on my end," Patch replied. "It's not my fault they weren't what you wanted."

"Be reasonable, Mr. G," Coulter said. "We've all failed here and none of us should bear the whole loss."

He showed Patch a small pistol that he'd kept concealed in the palm of his hand. "So hand over the money," he demanded in a threatening tone.

With no change of expression, Patch shrugged and took the envelope out of his pocket. Opening it, he took out one of the thousand dollar bills.

"This'll take care of my time and expenses."

He handed the envelope to Coulter and pocketed the bill. After considering this development for a moment, the antiquities dealer shrugged and accepted the envelope.

Braxton and Justin entered the room. Justin was rubbing his wrists where the rope had been tied.

"Now we'll take our leave, but I'm afraid you'll have to get along somehow without your fall guy."

"No matter," Patch said. "I'll just move to Plan B."

"I'll leave the forgeries to you, as a little souvenir of our time together," Coulter said as he and Braxton headed out the front door, followed by Kyoto and Justin who gave him one last dirty look. Patch stood at the door and watched them leave.

The men walked out the front gate and got in the white Cadillac convertible.

Patch immediately pulled out his phone and made a call. Kathleen watched him from across the room, unsure of what to expect.

"Hello," Patch spoke into the phone. "Is Sergeant Roybal there? This is Geronimo."

As he waited, he eyed Kathleen and the Twins, smiling.

"Sam, I know you're up to your ass in alligators getting ready for Indian Market, but I've got the information I promised you. Uh, huh. Just listen."

"The party responsible for the murder of Jonathan Morgan is a guy named Ryan Coulter. I told you about him. Remember? He has a small gang of goons working for him and they're all armed. One of them, a kid named Justin, is the one who actually pulled the trigger. That's right.

"And that Japanese fellow, Kyoto, is with them. But you'll have to move fast. They're headed out of town now in a white Cadi convertible. On their way to Paris, I believe. Oh, and you'll also want to stop by five-thirty-five Canyon Road to pick up another package. Good luck."

Patch clicked off the call and took a long slow deep breath. Then he turned to face Kathleen.

"Coulter's gonna tell the cops all about us when they find him," he told her. "And they'll be showing up here. So let's hear the rest of the story. Fast."

He picked up the black bag and began putting the statues inside.

"Can't we get out of here before they come?" Kathleen asked.

"We're not going anywhere. So talk. You can start with the first day you came to my office. What's the real reason you wanted Morgan followed?"

"I already told you," she replied. "I suspected him of betraying me, and I wanted to find out for sure."

Patch finished placing the statues in the bag, turned and took a step toward Kathleen. She kept the table between herself and the detective.

"That's the first lie," he said angrily. "I think you wanted him out of the way before the Twins showed up so you wouldn't have to share the loot with him. Am I right?"

She didn't answer.

"Am I right?" he demanded again, loudly.

"No, I just thought if he saw someone following him, he might be frightened away. That's all. You must believe me."

"Willy's not the smartest man alive, but I know he's not clumsy enough to be seen during a tail. I bet you told Morgan he was being followed. Didn't you?"

He stepped toward her menacingly. She pulled back.

"Didn't you?" he barked.

"All right. I told him. Yes, but I wouldn't have said anything if I thought he would shoot your partner. You gotta believe me."

Patch began to circle the table to get closer to her. She retreated from him, circling the table away from him.

"I don't believe he did shoot my partner. He'd had enough experience not to be blind-sided like that, up a dark alley with his gun still in his holster."

Patch circled the table in the opposite direction. Kathleen followed suit.

"But he would've gone up there with you," Patch continued. "You and your damsel-in-distress act. You could've stood as close to him as you like, and then put a bullet or two in his chest."

They stopped circling. Kathleen turned her back to Patch and began crying.

"No, Patch, I'm not like that. I would never—."

He flew around the table grabbing her by the wrist. He was angry, forceful.

"Cut the crap. I'm not buying the school-girl routine. Why'd you shoot him? Why?"

He shook her, and she stopped resisting him. Her body drooped in resignation.

"I didn't mean for Willy to get hurt," she said in a low voice. "Honest. But I was desperate. I thought if Willy caught up to us, and he thought Morgan was hurting me, he'd shoot him. So I put on an act. But Willy didn't shoot. Morgan shot him instead."

"And it was only after Morgan showed up dead that you knew Coulter's boys were in town. Is that it?"

She nodded.

"So you came back to me for protection?" he continued.

She nodded again, pathetically. She pulled Patch to her, looking up at him with big soulful eyes.

"Yes, but I would've come back to you anyway. I knew the very first moment I saw you—."

"Aren't you forgetting something?" Patch asked coldly. "Like this husband of yours? I've already got one married girlfriend. I'm not in the market for another one."

"Payton and I have had this on-again-off-again relationship for years. But it's over. He dumped me after he got his hands on the Twins. It sounds like you're about to do the same."

"Tough luck, huh?"

A tear came to her eye. She blinked it away.

"But I thought I meant something to you."

"Maybe I thought you did, once, for about a minute," Patch replied. "But now I know I could never trust you. You've got a complicated, scheming mind, always looking for other possibilities. I'd be looking over my shoulder all the time."

They heard the sound of a car pulling up outside.

"I think your ride's here," Patch said quietly.

Kathleen panicked trying to break free. Patch clamped down tight on her arm. She struggled harder.

At that moment, Lieutenant Johnson, Sam Roybal and another detective entered the gallery. Kathleen gave up the fight.

"Hello, Patch," Sam said. "Didn't expect to find you here."

"Hello, Sam. Did you get 'em?"

"They're being picked up as we speak. Out south on Cerrillos Road."

"Here's one more for your collection," Patch said as he pushed Kathleen away from him.

The other detective grabbed her by the arm. She shot daggers at Patch with her eyes.

"She helped get Willy shot," Patch continued. "And she and her husband figure in Luther Seumptewa's shooting, too. But the husband's whereabouts are unknown."

He pulled a thumb drive from his pocket.

"You'll find a recording of his voice on this tape, from when he set me up for a little scare on the Hill of the Martyrs."

Then he pulled a thousand dollar bill out of another pocket.

"And here's a thousand dollars Coulter tried to bribe me with."

Motioning toward the table, Johnson asked, "What's in the bag?"

"That's what all the fuss was about," Patch replied. "A couple of wooden statues that belong to the Zunis. I'm to deliver them to a tribal priest today for a ceremony."

They're fakes," Kathleen said. "Why bother?"

"Only the stones are fake, sweetheart," Patch explained. "The statues are authentic. I had the gems switched out before they left St. Louis, just in case they fell into the wrong hands."

Another shocked look spread across Kathleen's face.

"Then what did my husband get away with?"

A couple of logs with crudely carved faces."

Kathleen shook her head in disbelief.

"This town's gonna drive me nuts before it's all over," Johnson said, shaking his head.

"What's the matter, Lieutenant?" Patch grinned. "You look heart-broken. Did you think you had me?"

The three cops headed out the door with Kathleen in tow. Patch picked up the black bag and started to follow. Johnson paused, allowing Patch to catch up to him.

"Do me a favor," Johnson said. "In the future, why don't you stick to divorces and marital disputes?"

Patch winked and smiled.

"Sorry Lieutenant, but I've decided to expand my horizons. I think I'll make the recovery of stolen tribal artifacts a permanent part of my investigational operations. I might even take out an ad in the yellow pages. It might read: Eagle Eye Investigations. Solving murders, recovering stolen artifacts, receiving messages from the Spirit World."

"I was afraid of that," Johnson said as they parted company.

"I mean this case has really got my blood pumping again." Patch continued speaking to no one in particular. He walked to his bike and strapped the black bag on the back.

"I think I can even finish that painting that's been sitting in the corner."

He started the bike's engine, put it in gear and headed back down Canyon Road toward his apartment.

It was Saturday morning and Indian Market was, no doubt, getting underway. Patch took the side roads and back streets to avoid the crowds as he thought of getting some well-deserved shut eye.

He made his way to the Butterfly Gallery and delivered the Twins into the hands of a very grateful Abe.

11 Chapter Eleven

While Patch slept, the Plaza buzzed with activity. A thousand American Indian artists were set up to show and sell their creations to the eighty thousand tourists and buyers who'd come to town. It was an artistic tradition that was almost one hundred years old.

Patch awoke from his lengthy nap around three o'clock in the afternoon. He opened his window to get some fresh summer air. The vibrant sounds of Art Market filtered in to his apartment as he showered and dressed.

When Patch arrived at the Butterfly Gallery, a small crowd of specially invited guests had gathered for a very special event. In the center of the gallery's main room, Abe Seumptewa prepared to perform the cleansing ritual for the Guardians.

Patch found Jessie who stood next to Willy and Luther, both seated in wheelchairs. The two men, looking as though they'd just returned from war, were in arm-slings and bandages. A surly-looking nurse stood guard over them.

Abe stepped into the middle of the room, next to the table that held the familiar black bag.

"Normally, this kind of ceremony is held in private to protect our religion and our people," he told the crowd. "But the spirits have instructed us to begin a new process of sharing our ways more openly. At first I found this hard to accept, but I realized that it was the spirits who had instructed our elders to hide the ceremonies away in the first place. So if they've decided to bring them out again, so be it."

He began the ceremony. He turned to the Twins and spoke to them in Zuni, then began a lengthy prayer song.

Patch listened patiently, respectfully, as Abe droned on in his native tongue. Preachers and medicine men can go on forever, Patch thought and chuckled to himself.

Finally Abe reached the climax of the ceremony. He bent down and embraced the black bag lying on a table. Clutching the bag to his cheek, he whispered a short Zuni prayer, as a parent would whisper words of comfort to a lost child.

He then circled the room, repeating the chant. He paused near the front door, where an offering of cornmeal had been strewn on the floor, leading outside.

"We are leaving now, to take our brothers home," Abe announced. "They will be placed in a secret shrine on Corn Mountain where they can resume their work of protecting our tribe and the world. Farewell."

Two Zuni elders opened the gallery door, and Abe exited. A throng of people followed. Patch, Jessie, Luther and Willy remained inside.

"Luther, tell Patch and Jessie how you got away from Sykes," Willy suggested.

Luther chuckled.

"Old Indian trick," he said. "I told him that the War Gods were angry for being kidnapped. He didn't know that I had the fakes. I said they'd put a hex on him unless he allowed me to perform the Zuni Dance of the War Gods.

"Dance of the War Gods. What's that?" Jessie asked.

"Something I just made up," Luther replied. "That's what we always did to get rid of anthropologists and such. They'll believe anything."

"Clever," Patch said.

"Anyway, he believed me because he'd heard the rumors about the Twins' special powers," Luther continued. "So I told him that the dance had to be performed in the Santa Fe Plaza because that was an ancient Pueblo Indian burial ground. By that time, he was real spooked, and he fell for it, hook, line and sinker."

"So when did you take the bullet?" Patch asked.

"When he stopped the car and let me out, I took off running like hell towards your office. He must've thought it was part of the dance, cause he didn't catch on 'til I got around the corner. That's when he came after me with his guns a-blazin'."

He laughed, and they all laughed with him.

"Mr. Seumptewa," the nurse interrupted. "It's time for you and Willy to get back to the hospital."

"Okay, Nurse Ratchet," Luther joked. "Wheel us back to the loony bin."

She frowned at him as she prepared his wheelchair.

"Well, Geronimo, we're all real proud of you," Luther said. "If it wasn't for you, we might never have gotten the Twin Brothers safely back to Zuni."

He shook Patch's hand.

"Thanks, Luther, but we all did it together," Patch said modestly.

The nurse approached Willy's wheelchair.

"Nurse, I know you're doing your duty and all, be we need Willy for a little while longer. We have to—."

He thought hard for a moment before continuing.

"We have to perform a traditional Pueblo cleansing ceremony for him. That's it. He's been polluted by the evil bullets that were inside him."

"Well, I'm supposed to transport him back to the hospital," the nurse objected.

"It's an Indian religious thing. The spirits will be real mad if we don't do this. They might cause you or the medical doctor some harm. I promise to bring him straight back to the hospital when we're all done."

"Oh, all right," she said. "But have him back before eleven o'clock. Otherwise, I'll get my butt chewed."

She smiled for the first time.

"Deal," Patch said, and the nurse started pushing Luther's wheelchair toward the door.

"Come down to Zuni and see me some time," Luther called back to them. "I'll show all our hot Zuni Pueblo night spots."

They laughed as Luther waved goodbye and was whisked away.

"Boy, do I feel good," Patch proclaimed.

"Yeah, sometimes there's nothing like doing the right thing for the right reason," Jessie said with an air of smugness.

"Well, yes, there's that," Patch admitted, "but there's also this."

He fished around in his side jacket pocket and came up with a small object wrapped in tissue. As he peeled back the paper, Willy and Jessie came closer. What they saw was a very large diamond.

"Wow! Where'd you get that?" Willy asked.

"From Abe, as payment for guarding the Guardians."

He handed the stone to Willy, then began pushing his friend's wheelchair toward the door. Jessie walked beside Patch.

"The Zunis got all the precious stones that had been glued to the Twins for their tribal treasury," Patch explained.

"Gee, I love happy endings," Jessie said.

The threesome left the gallery and walked down the sidewalk towards the Plaza.

"I don't know what the Zunis are going to do with their gems," Patch mused. "But we're going to use ours to get some new furniture and tech gear for the office. What do you think of that?"

"How about a company car?" Willy's eyes were as sparkly as the diamond. "And another computer! I could be in charge of Internet research or something."

"Don't forget. You promised me a raise," Jessie scolded.

They paused. Willy handed the diamond back to Patch who stuffed it in his jacket pocket.

"Sure thing. No sweat. It's a big stone, so all that's possible," Patch promised. "But how about dinner at the Coyote Cafe, for now? On me."

Willy and Jessie both nodded with excitement like a couple of kids being promised ice cream cones. As they resumed their stroll, Jessie quietly slipped her arm around Patch's arm.

"It looks like you charmed your way through another tight one, Johnny," Jessie said.

"You know, guys, I really do feel like a new man," Patch replied. "From now on you're gonna see a new J.J. Geronimo. The first thing I'm gonna do is stay clear of married women."

Willy and Jessie just looked at one another in disbelief.

"No really, guys, I mean it," Patch protested. "If you don't believe me, just watch. And I'm going to start painting again."

As they walked on towards the Coyote Cafe, Santa Fe's downtown adobe skyline was just beginning to take on those famous orange and magenta hues painted by another New Mexico sunset.

And the magic of another Santa Fe night was about to begin.

ABOUT THE AUTHOR

Gary Robinson, a writer, artist and filmmaker of Choctaw and Cherokee Indian descent, has spent more than twenty-five years working with American Indian communities to tell the historical and contemporary stories of Native peoples in all forms of media.

His television work has aired on PBS, Turner Broadcasting, Ovation Network, and others. His non-fiction books, <u>From Warriors to Soldiers</u> and <u>The Language of Victory</u>, reveal little-known apsects of American Indian service in the U.S. military from the Revolutionary War to modern times.

He is also the author of several teen novels in the *PathFinders* series published by Native Voices Books. This unique series features Native American teen main characters who go on adventures and rediscover the value of their own tribal identities. (www.NativeVoicesBooks.com)

His children's books include <u>Native American Night Before Christmas</u> and <u>Native American Twelve Days of Christmas</u>, published by Clearlight Books of Santa Fe.

He lives in rural central California. More information about the author can be found at www.tribaleyeproductions.com and www.youtube.com/tribaleyepro. Follow him on Facebook at www.facebook.com/tribaleyepro.

www.ingramcontent.com/pod-product-compliance
Lightning Source LLC
Chambersburg PA
CBHW070332130626
46556CB00007B/2816